Out of control

He watched, helpless as the plane skidded on one ski like an out-of-control ice skater. It began turning — a spread of spruce trees coming up fast. The Cessna caromed off a boulder, the left ski and strut tore away. The wing tip grazed a tree and the plane lurched leftward into a spruce. A branch shattered the cockpit window.

He felt himself hurled forward.

Blackness . . .

Other Scholastic paperbacks
you will enjoy:

Avalanche
by Arthur Roth

Trapped
by Arthur Roth

The Iceberg Hermit
by Arthur Roth

Sole Survivor
by Ruthanne Lum McCunn

Young Man in Vietnam
by Charles Coe

Just a Little Bit Lost
by Laurel Trivelpiece

Yukon Journey

Frank McLaughlin

SCHOLASTIC INC.
New York Toronto London Auckland Sydney

ISBN 0-590-43538-8

12 11 10 9 8 7 6 5 4 3 2 1   1 2 3 4 5 6/9

Printed in the U.S.A.   01

First Scholastic printing, February 1991

I am grateful to Joe Muff, President of Alkan Air, for introducing me to two fellow Yukoners who were invaluable in my research: Monty Alford, a mountaineer and geohydrologist, whose book *Yukon Water Doctor* vividly recounts his experiences on the lakes and rivers of the territory; and Moe Grant, who gave me my first float plane flight, and whose own adventure as a bush pilot is more heroic than the story I've told here.

My wife, Ruth, graciously urged me to go to the Yukon at a time we could least afford the journey. Louise DeSalvo, Ned Eckhardt, Ron Kase and Robert Geller read sections of this work. Their friendship and encouragement enrich my life. Two pilot friends, Ed Veronelli and Al Harriman, with patience and good humor, answered dozens of questions about the wind, weather and VFR flying.

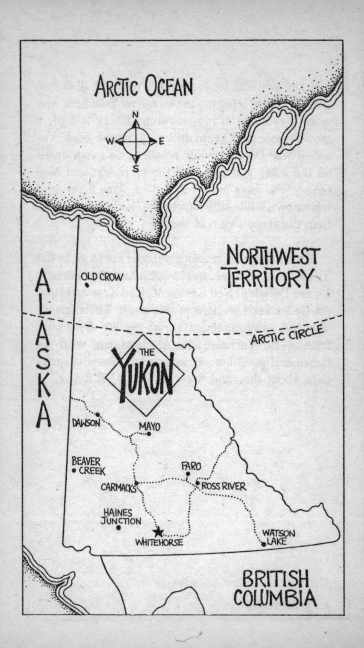

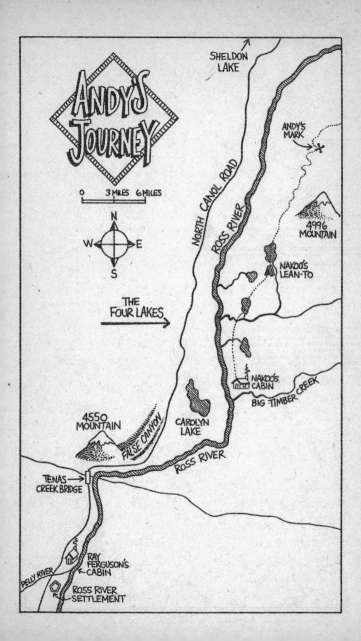

Prologue

The Yukon Territory is the northwestern corner of Canada that borders Alaska. The upper third of the triangular country, mostly barren tundra, is within the Arctic Circle. Below this frigid expanse is a different wilderness: mountain country with vast forests, powerful rivers and hundreds of lakes, many unnamed and some unvisited by humans. Wolves, bears and moose roam the empty land; and caribou outnumber people by seven to one. The entire population of the territory would not fill half of a modern sports stadium.

The airplane is integral to the Yukon. The bush pilots who fly them contend each day with swiftly changing weather, dangerous terrain and primitive landing conditions. For sixty years they have flown the mail, people and supplies between the tiny human outposts spread throughout Alaska and the Yukon. For the past forty years they have also ferried those who hunt, fish and prospect around the spectacular land. This is the story of one bush pilot and his son — who was afraid. . . .

Chapter 1

Snow came early to the Yukon. By the first week of November, eight inches were on the ground at Ross River. The small settlement — a general store, hotel, mission, school and a few houses — set on a plateau between the rugged Pelly Mountains was usually drier. The settlement at the foot of the mining country — a predominantly native community — was once a trading post called "Nahanni House."

Andy Ferguson stood looking out at the leaden sky through the window of the school's book room. He had been late this morning and had not had time to check his weather gauges. There had been a time when his father kidded him about the weather stats he recorded. His father used to call him the "weather bug," and bragged to Billy John, his mechanic, and Axel, the inn owner, how accurate his son's weather information was. Andy had felt good about it because his father was a pilot and misreading the weather could mean disaster. On weekends when his father was scheduled to fly, Andy still wrote weather notes for his father, which he left by their two-way radio.

Andy's eyes suddenly began watering. He wiped his sleeve across his eyes, glancing back at the door to see if anyone was watching. No, he was alone.

It was lunchtime. Miss Swenson, who knew Andy loved to read, let him eat in the book room. They had forty minutes before afternoon classes began. Normally, he read or did homework while he ate his bag lunch, but for the past two weeks he had been too jumpy. Andy went back to the table and tried to eat the remaining half of the peanut butter and jelly sandwich without gagging. Once he had liked peanut butter and jelly. But his grandmother, Nedda, had made the same sandwich two or three times a week since school had started. When he had told Nedda he was tired of the same stuff every other day, she had not understood. Andy wondered if it was because of the stroke she had suffered four years ago. He had no idea what a stroke was. That was the trouble. No one told him anything.

Andy knew he had to talk with someone. But who? His father was either away or when he was home did not want to talk. For the past two weeks Andy had looked for an opening, but none came. His father had been home the last three nights, but was busy with his ledger or was in his room. Who else was there? He wouldn't see Nakoo until Thanksgiving and Brian was gone.

That's why he was in such trouble. If Brian were here, there would be two of them. Charlie Redfox wouldn't be after him. Brian had been his only friend in Ross River. They had sat side by side in school, did their homework together and were always at each other's house. But Brian's mother couldn't stand living in such a remote place. She had convinced Brian's dad, who was some type of mineral expert, to return to British Columbia. They had left Ross River before school started this year.

Andy was failing two subjects. That was the easiest part to tell. At least he could explain why he was having trouble. But how could he explain about Charlie bullying him?

Andy was fifteen. Charlie was a year younger, but he was also a head taller and fifty pounds heavier. The first time Charlie came after him was near school, and the gym teacher had pulled Charlie off him before he had gotten hurt. Andy had no idea why Charlie attacked him.

The second time Charlie had caught him. It was two weeks ago, three days before he was cut from the basketball team. After practice, Andy had taken a shortcut across a field. Charlie and two of his friends chased and tackled him. He could have outrun Charlie, but not the three of them. Charlie had punched him in the face and arms; Andy had been knocked down three times. The third time he didn't get up. Charlie had kicked and cursed him while the other two kids scattered his books and sneakers around the field. Andy had limped home with a split lip and several cuts and bruises on his face and arms.

Andy's father had not been home that night. The next day Andy had returned home from school, stiff and sore. That evening his father had not noticed he had been beaten up and Andy had felt too ashamed to say anything. Now, he realized he should have said something.

Andy forced himself to eat the three vanilla cookies Nedda had packed, then crumpled the wax paper and half-eaten sandwich into the lunch bag. He walked next door to the bathroom, dropped the bag in the trash can, then looked at himself in the mirror over the wash basin. A thin, lightly freckled face stared back at him. "Fifteen years old, and less than a hundred pounds," he said aloud. He held up his small, white hands to the mirror and examined them — so different from his father's dark, weathered hands with their perfectly rounded nails. He felt pathetic.

Andy returned to the book room. He looked up at the clock by the door. Two minutes before the buzzer sounded; two minutes before afternoon classes began. Andy stood looking at the large map of the Yukon under the clock. He loved maps, and often pored over this one, sounding out the names of the lakes and rivers of the territory where he lived. But the map couldn't help him now. All he could think about was what would happen after school today. Would he have to run from Charlie again?

Chapter 2

Andy's father, Ray Ferguson, who was not scheduled to fly that day, sat alone at a table finishing a sandwich. He had spent the last two days at his cabin preparing for winter and feeling restless. After repairing a storm window and splitting some wood, he had driven his pickup truck to Ross River to loan it to Billy John. Billy, the mechanic who worked on his plane, wanted to stock his trapper's cabin with provisions and check his traps. The cabin was forty miles east of Ross River on the way to Faro. It would be an overnight trip. After he had helped Billy load the pickup, he had had Billy drop him at the inn.

The few tables in the motel's cafe were a familiar niche; finding a similar eating place in this desolate country would have required flying more than a hundred miles.

Ray Ferguson flew people and supplies to small settlements with names like Pelly Crossing, Beaver Creek and Old Crow. A handful of gravel roads connect these remote outposts, but planes were the lifeblood of the Yukon. Ray became so absorbed in this life he only returned to the states twice: his sister's wedding, his mother's funeral.

None of the regulars were there, and Axel, the inn's owner, had his annual fall cold and was upstairs wheezing and sneezing. Martha, Axel's wife, returned from the kitchen and poured coffee into Ray's half-empty cup. She then brought her own cup of tea and sat down across from him. Martha had been his wife's closest friend in Ross River. His wife, Sara, had died unexpectedly seven years ago; neither of them had recovered from her loss. They sat in silence. A log in the wood-burning stove across the room hissed, then made a popping sound.

Suddenly the front door opened and a moment later Father Dessault appeared in the cafe doorway. The gray-haired fifty-year-old priest was out of breath from the two-block walk from the mission. "Good to see you, Martha," he said, as he removed his black coat. He draped it over the chair next to Ray's and sat down across from the pilot. "I was hoping to find you here," he said to Ray as he ran his index finger under the white collar above his cassock. Martha returned with coffee for the priest.

"Need help," he said to Ray. "There's an outbreak of flu at the Indian camp by Sheldon Lake; two older people . . . dead."

Ray pushed the sugar across the table and replied, "No landing strip there, but there's a good field between Sheldon and Lewis Lakes."

"Could your partner fly up there from Watson Lake?" the priest asked. "They've got medical supplies."

"Eric sent the Beaver in for overhaul a week ago."

The priest thought for a moment, running his index finger along his trim, graying beard. "If I could get hold of some antibiotics, could you fly 'em over?" Ray nodded and they both looked out a window. The priest asked, "Will the weather hold?"

"Let's hope so," Ray answered, reaching for his jacket. "We'd better move, less than three hours of light left."

Father Dessault gulped down his coffee, stood up and put his coat on. Ray quickly paid the bill, and as they walked outside, said, "Billy's got my truck."

"No problem," Father Dessault replied. "We'll take the mission van. My keys are on the desk," he added, giving Ray a pat. "Pick me up at the nurse's place." Ray watched the priest walk stiffly across the street; it was obvious his arthritic knees were bothering him. Ray jogged to the mission office, found the keys and minutes later was waiting in the van in front of the nursing station.

Moments later, Father Dessault came out the door smiling, holding three vials. "Left over from the batch they sent us from Whitehorse," he said, opening the door on the passenger side. They drove the two miles out to Ray's place, the priest insisting he'd help Ray gas up.

Ray's landing field was set back on a rise about a hundred and fifty yards from the Pelly River. A road crew friend with a bulldozer had leveled it for him a few weeks after he and Sara had moved here.

Andy's father returned the favor two months later by flying a crib and baby accessories from White-horse to the machine operator. At the corner of the east end of the field was a rusting, yellow, corrugated metal shed. A hundred feet behind it, down a path, the Ferguson cabin was nestled among the spruce trees.

As the pickup stopped by the shed, Father Dessault looked over at Ray's Cessna 180 and asked, "When did you switch to skis?"

"Saturday," Ray replied, opening the shed. "Billy John gave me a hand." The two men each carried a five-gallon drum over to the single engine four seater. "With over six inches down and ice starting to form, no sense in leaving the floats on."

Fifteen minutes later Ray began warming up the Cessna's Continental engine. Because the temperature had hovered above freezing the last three days it was not necessary to warm the oil or use the cowling tent. Father Dessault reached the small package through the open cabin door that Ray secured under the passenger seat belt. Ray shouted above the noise of the propeller, "There's a radio tube on the table I picked up for Nakoo; could you grab it for me?"

Father Dessault turned and headed toward the pilot's home. As Ray waited, he put on his headset and radioed Ross River Airport. Ernie, who operated the radio from his wheelchair at the primitive facility, immediately answered. Ernie informed him that a low pressure front was moving in and snow had been reported southwest of Ross River. Ray quickly gave his flight plan: He'd pass over Jackfish

Lake and would land between Lewis and Sheldon Lakes. The trip should take just under an hour. He would try to make radio contact at Jackfish Lake on return and drop off the radio tube to Nakoo if the weather held. Father Dessault returned just as Ray received clearance.

The priest had a funny look on his face. He handed Ray the tube and shook his head. "I forgot Nedda was there; she gave me a start."

Ray laughed. "Your hair's white enough as it is," he said, closing the door and adjusting his headset.

As Father Dessault waved, Ray taxied the single engine plane to the east of the field, then headed back into the wind. He negotiated the turn carefully. Ross River was twenty-two hundred feet above sea level with mountains on three sides. Ray brought the Cessna around slowly, set his heading for northeast, adjusted the trim and five minutes later passed over False Canyon.

Familiar landmarks were blotted out by the white snow cover. He would fly lower than usual to maintain visibility. Carolyn Lake was in front of him, off to the left. He banked right and headed to where Big Timber Creek joined Ross River. Dropping another two hundred feet he looked ahead toward his friend Nakoo's place. Three miles later he passed over Nakoo's small log cabin. A wisp of smoke arose from the stove pipe; Nakoo or his wife, Edna, often came out when they heard Ray's plane. Not today.

Snow began to dot the windshield as he eased the rudder left to return to follow the river and his designated heading. Patches of open water on the river were the only sure markings. The engine sounded rough. He decided to switch gas tanks. A gust of wind shook the plane, pushing it rightward. Ray tightened his seat belt. The change in tank had not helped. He checked the altimeter: thirty-four hundred feet. He'd better take her higher. He lost sight of the river, but knew it was off to his left. He pushed the throttle for more power, trying to gain altitude.

The plane did not respond; the engine began making a coughing sound. Ray's heart beat faster. The fuel line must be clogged. He would have to put her down. But the plane was losing power and could not buck the crosswind. The Cessna yawed like a rowboat in heavy seas. The gauges danced in front of his eyes. He was on a roller coaster now. The plane dropped from under him, and his hand flew up, hitting metal. He was being blown away from the river into the mountains.

Ray groped for, found and turned the dial to his radio and called, "Mayday, mayday . . . Cessna Charlie, Lima X-Ray," he stopped, his breath taken away by another elevatorlike plunge downward. "Niner one, fifteen miles northeast of Carolyn Lake." The radio crackled; he heard something indistinct. It didn't matter. The propeller stopped and the Cessna was powerless. He could barely see out the windshield.

The plane was impossible to control. Each sharp gust jolted the aircraft into a precarious new angle. It wanted to tumble. He opened the window to get a better view. Squinting through the swirling snow, he caught a glimpse of spruce trees under him and to his left. It was silent. The plane steadied and glided. Then, creaking and shuddering, it toppled right and made a quarter turn. For a moment the passenger window was halfway below him. He could see a ridge. He was barely above the trees. Lowering the left aileron brought the aircraft level.

Ray held his breath. The ridge was directly in front. He tried to ease the nose up. Then an updraft carried him up and over. He let out a breath. An uneven slope appeared to his right. He fought to steady the plane. Through the snowflakes, he could see a passageway between trees and scrub. He lowered his flaps, brought the nose up a fraction and his right ski caught snow. The craft bounced, then the right ski hit hard as it touched rock beneath it.

Ray tried to bring the left ski down, but the plane careened over snow-covered rock.

He watched helplessly as the plane skidded on one ski like an out-of-control ice skater. It began turning — a spread of spruce trees coming up fast. The Cessna caromed off a boulder, the left ski and strut tore away. The wing tip grazed a tree and the plane lurched leftward into a spruce. A branch shattered the cockpit window.

He felt himself hurled forward.

Blackness . . .

Chapter 3

The only thing Andy Ferguson liked about himself was his name. His father had named him after Andy Drummond, the pilot who had taught his dad to fly, and had helped him get his first job. His flight instructor had been killed in a plane crash the year before Andy was born.

Andy sat at his desk and looked over at Charlie. He guessed that Charlie and his friends had disliked Brian and him for some time, but he couldn't figure out why. He looked up at the clock.

An hour to go and school would be over. One more day and the week would end. Andy gazed out the window. He could barely keep his eyes open. Looking down at the open page of his workbook, he forgot which exercise had been assigned. Andy's desk was the fourth back in the row by the windows. Leslie, who had long blonde hair and was a year younger, sat in the next row, a seat in front. Andy daydreamed about Leslie constantly, but he was too timid to do more than mumble a few words to her once in a while. Even when he rehearsed what he would say, the words didn't come out right. Andy craned his neck to see her workbook, but she was turned the wrong way. They were the only two working on this exercise. Then he remembered that Miss Swenson had done the first two on the left-hand page for them.

There were thirteen kids in the warm classroom. In a regular school they would be in different classes; in this settlement school they were all mixed between kindergarten and ninth grade, except for Andy, the only tenth-grader. He wondered how Miss Swenson kept things straight.

Miss Swenson was the first teacher Andy had ever liked. She was soft-spoken and kind. He had never seen her flustered. He liked to watch her. She was tall, with dark hair and wore no makeup. Andy dreamed a lot about her, too. She was the only teacher who had ever complimented him — on a story he wrote — and she did not make fun of him.

Andy spent the afternoons in her class for English, reading and history. Because he was the only one in his grade, Miss Swenson had him do a lot of work on his own. Each Friday he had to turn in a report to her. One week she would pick a book, the next week he would pick one. He had turned an extra report in at the end of September. After that, she let him eat his lunch in the library — which at Ross River school was only a room with a desk, table and shelves of books. Everyone called it the book room. She sometimes let him go there when he finished his classwork, too. Andy didn't mind writing the reports. Miss Swenson didn't mind his daydreaming.

But Mr. Harding did. Andy spent all morning with this balding, unsmiling man with the jutting jaw and the glasses halfway down his nose. Mr. Harding taught algebra, science and health. Andy was failing algebra and barely passing biology; he was the only student taking these subjects. Mr. Harding hollered at him every day, and said he didn't pay attention. Andy didn't understand a lot of what he read in the assigned chapters, but he was afraid to ask questions.

Last week when he had been looking out the window during a health lesson, Mr. Harding threw an eraser at him. It hit him in the neck. It didn't hurt, but Charlie and the other kids had hooted. He was glad Leslie had been absent that day. But she was there the next day when he had come to school with his pajama top on. Forgetting to fully dress was typical of stuff that happened to him lately.

It started to snow. Very lightly. What difference did it make? They hardly ever closed school. Many kids stayed home when the weather was bad or if the temperature fell more than twenty below. His father made him come no matter what. He looked up. Miss Swenson was marking papers at her desk in the front of the room. She looked up and smiled at him, then made a writing gesture with her hand, telling him to get back to work. He looked down and tried to figure out whether the underlined passage in the seventh sentence was a phrase or a clause. Andy finished another half dozen sentences and looked out again. The flakes were small but were coming down steadily.

A moment later he heard his name called. Miss

Swenson pointed to the door. The principal was there, beckoning with his index finger. What had he done? Andy followed the principal down the hall to the office. The principal picked up the phone receiver off his desk and handed it to Andy, saying, "Father Dessault."

Father Dessault told him that his father had had to put his plane down north of Carolyn Lake. He asked Andy to come over to the mission. Andy asked for and received permission to leave. He quickly returned to the classroom, told Miss Swenson there was an emergency, grabbed his jacket from the closet, his books from his desk and left. At least he wouldn't have to worry about Charlie today.

Andy quickly walked the block to the mission. He kicked the snow from his boots and went into Father Dessault's small office. The gray-haired priest still had his black coat on. He and Andy walked over to the large map taped on the wall. There were pins in it, indicating where the Catholic families in the district lived.

"What happened?" Andy asked.

"We don't know," the priest replied, his finger tracing a line up past Carolyn Lake. "Ernie, over at the airport, picked it up on the emergency frequency. He thinks your father's about fifteen miles northeast of the lake."

"Is he okay? What did he say?"

The priest shrugged. "Only gave his position. I can tell you where he was heading . . . Sheldon Lake."

Andy put his finger on the map, then moved his

15

finger down a bit. "It's not far from Nakoo's. Does Nakoo know?"

The priest shook his head no. "Your father was going to drop off a tube for his radio on the way back."

"We'll get him; I'll go to Nakoo's, then the two of us'll find him."

"Andy, Nakoo's over seventy."

"But he's an Eskimo, a trapper. He knows the country."

"How will you get there?"

"Can you help me?"

"Sure, if I can," the priest replied.

"Drive me back to the cabin. We'll put the snow-mobile on the pickup and you — "

Andy stopped; Father Dessault had held up his hands and shook his head. "Billy John has your father's truck," he interrupted, "and there's no way we can reach him. It won't fit in the van," he added, anticipating Andy's next question.

They both stood silently, then Father Dessault said, snapping his fingers, "Let's try Axel." He picked up the phone. Father Dessault talked with Axel at the motel, but the worn tires on the inn-keeper's pickup couldn't handle the snow.

Father Dessault frowned. "It's too late today. It'll be dark in another hour . . . besides, they'll send a search party for him in the morning."

"Father, how do you know the weather'll be better?"

The priest scratched his head, thinking for a moment. "All right," he said, walking over to his cluttered desk, "if the weather isn't better, go in the morning. I'll find someone to take you up to the turnoff. How far is it?"

"About twenty miles."

"I'll call you between eight and eighty-thirty tomorrow morning." The priest paused, then asked, "Are you sure you can find your way from there?"

"I hiked to Nakoo's twice last year."

"It's not the same in the snow," Father Dessault warned.

Andy knew that. Nakoo had told him stories about what happened to landmarks after it snowed. "The trail's well marked," Andy said, "and the last half of it runs right beside Big Timber Creek." The priest nodded. Andy picked up his books and opened the door. "Thanks, Father," he said. "I want to get home."

"I'll call you in the morning," Father Dessault said. "Let's hope the weather breaks."

Carrying two books in each hand, Andy jogged over the snow-covered streets and paths toward home. He tried to visualize what had happened to his father, and by the time he reached the cabin twenty minutes later, he had begun forming a plan.

Nedda, his grandmother, was wrapping bread on the counter by their big wood-burning stove. Nedda, who was a quarter Athapaskan Indian, did not speak, and had come to help his mother shortly before his sister was born. But the baby was stillborn. The next day Andy's mother lapsed into a coma and died hours later. His father had been away. Nedda had been with them ever since.

Andy took off his jacket and told Nedda what had happened. Again, Andy wondered how much the stroke had affected her. Since he was never sure how much she understood, he pantomimed the situation with his hands. Then he went over to his father's VHF radio, turned the transmitter on and gave his name and his father's call sign. He listened. Then he repeated himself.

There was a crackling sound, then Andy heard Ernie Wehrhausen's voice. "Ross River Airport, Wehrhausen, over."

"Any news on my father? Over."

"Negative, we can't raise him. Jackson Lake operator can't either, over."

"Could you give me his last transmission, over."

"Just his call sign, and fifteen miles northeast of Carolyn Lake. Acknowledge."

Andy repeated the position, thanked Mr. Wehrhausen and signed off.

"I'm going to Nakoo's," he told Nedda.

Nedda shook her head, pointing out the window at the snow. She took a pan from the stove and poured hot chocolate into a cup and handed it to Andy. Nedda was over sixty, had a weathered face, long straight gray-black hair and dark circles under her black eyes.

Andy took a sip of the steaming chocolate and assured her, "Tomorrow morning." She nodded.

Andy went into his father's room. He pulled the map box out by the double bed and rummaged through it until he found the Pelly River aeronautical map. Andy called Nedda over and showed her the route he would take. He would go about twenty miles up the North Canol Road that wound north then east, then take the trail circling around the southern part of Carolyn Lake to Nakoo's cabin. The cabin sat two hundred yards back on a promontory where Big Timber Creek joined Ross River. The light was dim so Andy took the flashlight they kept in a kitchen drawer and scanned the map with it. Using a ruler and pencil he carefully measured distances, and then after several minutes, penciled in an "x." "This is where he is," he said both to Nedda and himself. Then he measured it out again to check.

Andy looked up from the table. It was nearly dark. He could go over the map later; it was more important to check out the snowmobile now. Andy took a big gulp from the hot chocolate, grabbed the spare key hanging by the hook next to the door and headed for the shed. He went in and took the canvas off the engine section of the two-piece Bolin autoboggan. After moving the kerosene heater next to the engine, he lit the wick. Then he carefully mixed oil with the gas and used a funnel to pour the mixture into the tank. Deciding to warm the oil before starting the engine, he stepped back and bumped into Nedda. She had followed him out.

Andy looked at the worried expression on his grandmother's face.

"You can help me," he said. He opened the seat cover of the back section of the snowmobile and pretended to put things in it. She nodded, gesturing that she would help. Andy looked thoughtfully at Nedda. His mother had died when he was eight. Nedda had been with them for seven years. In all that time she had no interest in learning English, but he had learned to communicate with her quite well. Mostly they used sign language, and though she did not write, she understood many of the words he wrote.

Andy took an empty coffee can from a shelf and handed it to Nedda. He poured some oil into it. It was a familiar routine. Throughout the Yukon, after freezing weather came batteries were removed from cars, trucks and planes and kept inside; and engine oil was warmed before motors were started. Nedda returned to the cabin and heated the oil on the stove.

Ten minutes later Nedda returned with the oil and a jacket for Andy. He moved the kerosene heater aside, poured the warm oil in the case and tried to start the engine. On the third try, it coughed into action, sputtered then stopped. On the next try it took. While it idled, Andy went to the side of the cabin and checked his weather gauges. The barometric pressure was low; he had a feeling the weather was not going to change for a while. He returned to the shed, prepared a reserve can with the gas-oil mix, then shut off the engine. When he returned to the cabin it was dark. Nedda was preparing dinner.

Andy began laying out clothes and tools for the trip. Then he and his grandmother ate in silence.

Afterwards, he tore out a sheet from his notebook and made a list:

ax
matches
goggles
ski mask

thermos
food
clothes for me
clothes for dad
compass

Andy read each item to her, pausing between each to make sure she understood. She then went over to the wall and took down his snowshoes. He nodded. She also pantomimed that he'd better take rope. He added the two words to the list then went over and turned their radio on. Reception was very poor. He flipped around the dial. There was too much static to get the Whitehorse station. It had the strongest transmitter, since Whitehorse was the capital of the Yukon Territory and the only community that was considered more than a settlement. Finally, he was able to tune in the Watson Lake station. Watson Lake was the settlement more than two hundred miles southeast of Ross River; it was just above the British Columbia border. After straining to listen for twenty minutes, all Andy could determine was that it wasn't snowing there, but that the storm extended from the Alaskan border and was blanketing the central Yukon. Andy wondered if Eric Larrabe had heard that his father was down. Eric was his father's partner and BackCountry Air's other pilot. Eric flew out of Watson Lake. Andy knew Eric would fly up as soon as the weather cleared. Andy turned off the radio and looked around.

In the twenty-by-thirty-six-foot cabin they lived in, Andy had no privacy. His father's room was closed off by a door. Nedda's smaller space was screened by a two-piece blanket curtain she had made. When he was a little boy, Andy had liked the openness. Twice, when his father was away, he had awakened late at night and discovered the stove pipe glowing and pulsing. The first time had been when his mother was alive. She had stopped the pipe fire by closing off the air. The second time was after his mother had died; he had awakened Nedda who quickly put the fire out. Since then his father had changed the pipe (removing an elbow) and there had been no problem. Andy had asked his father for his own room more than two years ago.

His father had let him build an eight-by-ten room onto the side of the cabin. Andy had constructed it himself mainly out of logs. It even had a floor. His father had brought lumber back, along with an old window frame. Andy had moved his weather notebooks, magazines, mineral collection and personal stuff out there. He loved his "weather office," as his father called it, even though it was cold in the winter. When his father was gone on overnight trips Andy snuck the kerosene heater from the shed. He and Brian had liked to hang out in the office. He missed Brian a lot.

Taking his flashlight Andy went outside to the shed to check his weather gauges. The temperature was 28 degrees and the barometric pressure had not changed. He thought about his father. Was he alive? Huddled in the plane? At least it wasn't too cold. Andy looked up into the overcast night. The snow had stopped, but it might be several days before visibility improved. He made two trips to the woodpile and loaded the stove for the night.

Before going to bed, Andy decided to check the map one more time. Then he had an idea. He tore out a blank page from his notebook and carefully copied the section of the map from Nakoo's to where he thought his father might be. He enlarged the area trying to sketch everything to scale. It was amazing the detail he hadn't seen until he began drawing his own map. Andy glanced over at Nedda in her chair; she was knitting. She looked up and held up the burgundy colored wool. She wrapped the garment around her neck and pointed to him. She was making a scarf. He thanked her and put two more words on his list — "map" and "scarf."

He wasn't tired. He decided to read until he fell asleep. It didn't work. His mind kept wandering. He remembered the two times he had helped his father look for people in the wilderness. The first time Constable McCarthy had asked his father to look for an old trapper who had not checked in. That was up near Jackfish Lake, about fifty miles northeast of Ross River, the same way his father had flown today. Although it had taken two tanks of gas and most of a day, that search had not been hard. It had been the same time of year as now, only there had been no snow on the ground. The old man, who lived alone, had had a heart attack while returning from his trapline. Andy shivered when he remembered. It was the first time he had ever seen a dead person.

The second time had been late in the summer three years ago. A fishing party had not returned to their base camp for pickup. It had taken almost two days to find them. They had been canoeing along the Riddell River, north of Ross River, and had gotten lost among a group of unnamed lakes. Peering down from the plane, searching for people in that empty land wasn't easy. It always amazed him how his father could crisscross the country, fly in-between mountains, drop low over lakes and streams and not get lost. The second of those days was windy, and Andy had cracked the top of his head three times during periods of turbulence.

Andy wondered whether he would ever be brave like his father. He remembered Nakoo's story of when his father's plane had engine failure up near Granite Canyon near the MacMillan River, before Andy was born. His father had had two passengers and a wing tore off in the crash landing. His father had started the survival stove and made the shaken passengers stay with the plane while he hiked thirty miles to Pelly Crossing. The temperature had dropped to 20 degrees below zero during the trip. His father had returned the next day with another pilot to pick up his passengers.

Other stories flashed through his mind as he lay there: the new company pilot who had lost his life when he'd crashed about twelve miles from the lake camp where he had dropped a hydrologist and his assistant. The pilot survived the crash, was not badly hurt, and lived for twenty days. But snow had turned the landscape into a white maze, and the man could not find his way back to the camp. They had found his plane two weeks after it was reported missing, but not him; and a year passed before the pilot's clothing and remains were discovered.

At least now it was early November, Andy thought, and not too cold. If he could get to Nakoo's, he knew the old Eskimo would help him. But what if his father were rescued before they got there? His father would be angry that Andy risked his and Nakoo's lives traveling overland.

No. Andy wasn't going to sit in school wondering if his father were alive. He wasn't waiting for Father Dessault to call him either. He would take the snowmobile and go directly to Nakoo's. Before daylight he would begin the most important journey of his life.

Chapter 4

Ray Ferguson was dreaming. His wife, Sara, had heard his plane and come out of the cabin carrying a flaming pine tip. He saw her move quickly from wick to wick, lighting the pots along the runway field. One by one the lights blinked on. He circled into the wind and brought the plane down. He saw her face framed by the fur hood. She was standing in the cold by the end of the strip where he taxied over. He shut off the engine, stepped out of the plane and turned toward her. She was not there.

Then Ray jerked awake. Sara was dead. And he was freezing. He tried to move, but a stab of pain in his right shoulder stopped him. He was in his plane. Alive. His left eye was swollen shut. He could barely see. He lifted his left hand. It had no feeling when he touched his forehead with it. He clumsily rubbed his finger against his eyelid, brushing away matted blood. Now he could see with both eyes.

Ray's mind began to clear. He had to move fast. The plane was listing about ten degrees on its portside. As his eyes grew accustomed to the dark, he realized that a broken branch was jammed against his shoulder. The branch had plunged through the windshield and snapped.

He willed himself to act. He undid his seat belt. By pressing backward and downward against the seat and pushing the branch with his left hand he freed himself. Excruciating pain. His shoulder was obviously broken or dislocated. The effort sapped him. He would rest for a while. Dream of Sara.

Ray roused himself. If he fell asleep, he would freeze to death in minutes. He brought his left hand up and slapped his face. No feeling. He brought his left hand to his right hand and began rubbing it. His entire body was numb with cold. He could not feel his feet so he tried tapping them up and down on the plane's floor. Only one worked. His head hurt, but the only intense pain was in his shoulder. How long had he been unconscious? He had forgotten his watch. Maybe an hour. Ray realized he was close to shock.

Grunting and groaning he clambered and twisted his aching body between the front seats, then the backseats. Panting, he fell onto the floor and groped around, feeling for his survival gear. Thank God, he had not been carrying cargo. The gear was wedged in the back of the fuselage, wrapped in canvas. He winced, using both hands to undo the thong tie. He opened up the canvas and found his flashlight. He pushed the switch forward. No light. Then he remembered he had reversed the batteries to preserve them. It took a minute to unscrew the cap, reverse the batteries, then screw the cap back on. Everything he did hurt and was in slow motion.

He pushed the flashlight switch forward. He had

light. Feeling was coming back; his teeth began to chatter. He had to get warm. Fumbling around, he found the small can-stove Nakoo called a *koodlik*. He unpacked it, found his matches, lit it and wedged it so it would sit level. He wanted to climb into his sleeping bag but needed to do something about the pain first. Clumsily, he folded the canvas and climbed back to the front seat, jamming the canvas into the hole in the windshield to keep snow and cold air out. He worked his way back and sat down again. The can opener in his survival kit was nearly impossible to hold and turn with only one good arm. Finally, he opened a can and ate corned beef, then brushed snow into the empty can and heated it over the pot. Minutes later, with his parka pulled around him, he drank the foul tasting water and took three aspirins from the bottle in his first-aid kit.

The next half hour was agony, trying to untie and pull his boots off with his left arm. His right ankle was swollen and throbbing. Even though the cabin was starting to warm, his body continued to shake. A final wrench made him yelp in pain; the boot came free and he was able to crawl slowly into the sleeping bag. Weary and shaking, Ray turned on his left side and huddled in a fetal position. He shut off the flashlight. The only light in the cabin now was the flickering light of the tiny stove. He began to feel drowsy. He would think about Sara.

The images of his young wife began to blur as his body warmed. He had stopped shaking but ached all over. The images became confusing as he drifted into sleep.

Then Andy was standing there. Ray winced.

Andy was not born yet. Then he was awake.

He was warm but in great pain. A couple of hours must have passed. He reached outside the sleeping bag with his left hand, groping for the flashlight. The small survival stove had nearly burned itself out.

He would not need it the rest of the night. What he did need was more aspirin. Which meant another trip forward to get enough snow to melt for a sip of water. As he blindly felt around the cold, metal floor, he found the old Chicago Cubs baseball cap Andy had given him; he put it aside for later. Ray struggled out of the bag and slowly put on his parka and gloves. Each movement brought fiery pain to his shoulder and awareness of other bruises and lacerations. His knees ached, his right pant leg was torn and matted blood was visible on and under the khaki fabric.

He would make it now. His shoulder and ankle were probably broken. Maybe he had a concussion. Though he was still a bit groggy, he knew he wouldn't fall into shock. Poking through the canvas, he filled the empty can with snow from the plane's roof. It was not snowing now, but he felt that there must be at least three inches on the roof. He'd worry about that in the morning. The effort, scrambling fore and aft, had exhausted him. Wearily, Ray rooted out one of the three remaining candles Nedda had made for his kit and wedged it into the coffee can. He lit the wick, and by balancing his screwdriver and pliers on the lip, he was able to heat the smaller can that was filled with snow.

Ray felt dizzy as he waited for the snow to melt.

He began to think what he should do in the morning. What would the weather be like? Would a rescue party come? Who would it be? His partner and closest friend Eric had gone to Victoria, British Columbia, to spend two weeks with his wife's parents, while his plane was being overhauled. It was unlikely that Eric would even find out he had gone down. With the fishing and hunting season winding down two of his other pilot friends had signed on to do some charter work in Alaska. If his radio message got through, who would know?

Ray frowned. Ernie at the settlement's airstrip or Father Dessault would let Andy know. Ray shook his head. Andy was an enigma to him. His son had been a bright little boy, always smiling, avid for adventure. But over the past five years the boy had grown sicklier and withdrawn. Twice in the last years he had gone over to school to discuss Andy's listlessness. The teachers agreed that Andy was intelligent but frittered away his time daydreaming.

Ray took three more aspirins from the plastic container, washing them down with the greasy snow water. His head ached, his entire body was sore, but at least he was warm. He shut off the flashlight but decided to leave the candle burning. It would hold down the cabin chill and he had two in reserve. He crept back into the sleeping bag. Sleep would heal him, turn off the pain.

But sleep wouldn't come. He thought of his own father, a successsful Chicago stockbroker, who had left him, his mother and sister to marry his secretary. He wondered, at times, how much his contempt for his father had to do with his becoming a bush pilot. The year he and Eric started Back-Country Air he realized that it was men like his father who helped keep him in business; they made enough money to afford the hunting and fishing trips to the Yukon and the Northwest Territories. Even his love of Canada and the Far North had begun when his father had taken the family on a trip to Lake Winnipeg.

Ray Ferguson shook his head. He did not want to think about his own father. What was wrong with his son? He shifted in the sleeping bag to ease the throbbing of his ankle. The pain was subsiding a bit. He had gotten so frustrated last year he had asked Doc Sinnickson from Whitehorse to examine Andy on one of his twice-monthly visits to Ross River. The doctor could find nothing wrong.

What would Andy do? He pictured his hapless son. And silent Nedda. Then he knew. Andy knew weather and the way to Nakoo's. His son also handled the snowmobile well. Andy loved Nakoo. The old Eskimo was like a grandfather to him. Andy would go to Nakoo. Ray muttered to himself, "Good old Nakoo."

Andy often spent weekends and holidays with Nakoo and his wife, Edna, at their remote cabin. Ray considered them family. He flew supplies to them each month and was happy that Nakoo still made a little money trapping and could fish as much as he wanted. Ray began to relax. Nakoo would find him. Minutes later he fell into a dreamless sleep.

Chapter 5

Andy looked at the clock again. Five forty-five A.M.
He felt like he hadn't slept. He had tossed and
turned most of the night, looking over at the clock
every half hour or so. After his feet touched the
cold floor, he was fully awake. Maybe he could get
out of there before Nedda got up. No. He saw her
blanket-curtain move, and she padded silently to
the kitchen. Andy dressed quickly.

During the next half hour Andy hurried back and
forth between the cabin and shed. It was snowing
lightly. The temperature was 17° and the barometer
was low. He had put the kerosene stove on to warm
the snowmobile engine and warmed some oil for the
case. He had packed the compartment under the
seat with the items he and Nedda had checked.
Andy needed a rifle, but it was his fault his father's
was gone. They would use Nakoo's. He would strap
the light Yukon Trailer snowshoes on his back.

Andy ate two of Nedda's sourdough biscuits and
packed another half dozen. He drank a cup of hot
chocolate and was ready to leave. He was surprised
when Nedda hugged him. He couldn't remember

the last time anyone had touched him. He hugged her back and told her he was only going into Ross River to wait for a ride. She wrapped the new scarf around his neck. Moments after he walked out the door, she called after him. He had left his father's ski mask on his chest of drawers.

The snowmobile started on the second try. He guided it out to the shed, felt for his goggles, adjusted the snowshoes on his back, closed the shed and eased the heavy autoboggan forward. He looked back and waved at Nedda, crossed the field his father used as his strip and headed for the road.

He was nervous and excited. The snow was a foot deep. He drove slowly. It was the first time he had used the machine since the winter before. He felt warm under his layer of clothes and decided not to use the goggles or ski mask until he had to. Andy turned onto the road. It was smoother, the snow less deep. It was also dark and he realized he would only be able to drive between five and ten miles an hour if he expected to stay on the road. He looked at his father's watch that he had strapped on his wrist; it was a few minutes before seven; almost two hours before daylight.

Andy shuddered, feeling the danger of what he was doing for the first time. The turnoff for Nakoo's was twenty miles away and he was barely out of Ross River now. He realized how hard it would be just to keep the snowmobile on the road. It was wide enough for two trucks to pass, but he was having difficulty seeing where the side of the road was.

He stopped, putting the engine on idle. He stood

up and walked over and brushed off a road sign; it indicated the old Ross River Indian village was off to his right. There were two access roads; he realized he had passed the first and had not seen it. He would have to stay alert and not be careless.

Andy racked his mind trying to recall the landmarks Nakoo had given him. He thought back to the trip he had made the summer before last. Another mile or so ahead was a big hill where a mountain was close in, then about two miles after that was an abandoned truck cab by the left side of the road; it wasn't far from another road sign. His biggest help would be the Tenas Creek Bridge, which was a third of the way to the turnoff. That was a half hour away. "Keep calm," he told himself.

It was snowing a little heavier when he started again. He stood, leaned forward and tried the goggles. They helped a little, but he had to wipe snow from them continually. He sighed. If only Sammy were with him. He would be okay if he still had his dog. It had been his fault that Sammy had been killed. No wonder his father had been angry. He lifted his goggles up on his forehead and kept going, grinding his teeth. He would do this. If he failed, it made no difference. He was nothing anyway.

Snow licked his eyes, making him blink. Andy shifted to a kneeling position. The next mile went smoothly. Keep steady, keep steady, he told himself. Through the hazy darkness he squinted. How far off the road was the abandoned truck cab? He hadn't passed it yet. Or had he? Andy shuddered, remembering the stories Nakoo had told him of people who had perished yards from safety because the snow had blotted out all that was familiar.

Andy jerked the steering wheel to the right; he had almost driven off the edge of the road looking for the truck cab. Drifts had made the sides of the road invisible. The tips of his fingers and toes were cold. Andy stopped the machine and lifted the snowshoes over his head, dropped them to the ground. He clapped his hands and jumped up and down. Then he opened the seat cover, unwrapped a biscuit, ate it and drank some hot chocolate. After adjusting the snowshoes on his back, he started forward again at jogging speed. The snow had stopped; he rode in a sitting position. Ten minutes later he was over the crest of a hill and starting down.

The snowmobile was going a little faster now. Then something hazy loomed in front. He slowed. It was the one-lane bridge over Tenas Creek. After crossing, Andy took out his map from his inside shirt pocket and with his flashlight on, looked for the next landmark. The road turned sharply right just ahead. In the darkness ahead was a mountain that rose forty-five hundred feet. He could not see it. He took off his gloves, blew on his hands, then sat down again. He eased the machine forward slowly and resumed his slow pace.

Peering intently into the darkness, Andy instinctively turned the hand control. The tip of the machine was off the road. Getting off the machine he tramped the snow firm at the side of the road then slowly brought the snowmobile around. Now he noticed a darker mass than the darkness around him. The mountain loomed in the direction he had been heading. He could make out the outline of the road ahead. According to the map he would have a straight six-mile run now, before the road angled left by False Canyon.

By keeping his eyes on the right side of the road, Andy kept the snowmobile cruising just under ten miles an hour. Snow provided the only illumination. Occasionally he could see patches of water when the river ran close to the road on his right side. He would feel more confident with light. The mountain was off to his left. He was heading east. Andy shifted from a kneeling position to a sitting position; the steady drone of the engine lulled him into a reverie about the first trip he had taken two summers back. Andy and his seven-year-old golden retriever, Sammy, had made an exciting overnight hike to Nakoo's cabin, walking the same route he was traveling now.

During that first day Sammy had bounded along all day with him. They had stopped several times along the river beside the North Canol Road, and Sammy had chased several squirrels and rabbits. Andy grew tired and began looking for a place to camp out. He found a good spot, protected by an overhanging rock on an embankment by the river. He had taken off his backpack when Sammy had suddenly darted out of sight. The dog normally returned after a few minutes.

An hour later Sammy was still not back. Andy had started a fire, heated some bean soup and ate two of the biscuits Nedda had packed. Then he had gone up the river a quarter of a mile, called for Sammy and went nearly the same distance the other way, and called again. No Sammy. Finally, he climbed into his sleeping bag and became more and more scared. The night then was twice as light as it was now. Andy heard wolves howling in the distance and some crashing about in the nearby woods. He called again and again. Somehow, despite his fear, he fell asleep.

Andy woke in a panic, feeling hot breath against his face. It was Sammy. He reached up and patted the dog, gave her the biscuit he had saved, and minutes later the dog was curled up against him. Andy slept soundly the rest of the night. The bright sun had awakened him early the next morning; they had reached Nakoo's in time for lunch. Two months later, because of him, Sammy would be dead. Andy felt his eyes tearing and tried to clear them.

Whoosh! Andy felt himself tumble off the seat. The cord yanked his neck as a snowshoe whacked the back of his head. Snow came up around him as the snowmobile turned on its side and skidded to a stop. Andy quickly jumped to his feet and stopped the engine. The road had very slowly angled left. Because he had been riding slowly, he had simply drifted off the road into a ditch. Neither he nor the machine was damaged. But could he turn the heavy engine section over? Andy unhitched the light back section, turned it over and dragged it back on the road. He was puffing from the exertion as he looked at the front section. Fortunately, it was not all the way over on its side.

Andy grabbed a snowshoe and began clearing snow from under the high side and around the rubber track. Then he began clearing in front of the machine. He put his snowshoes on and began tramping a path back to the road. He was less than five feet off the road, but he was panting heavily as he finished the pathway. At least his hands and feet were warm again.

Using his snowshoe he cleared more snow from under the tread and freed more crusted snow. He counted three and pushed with all his might. The front section dropped in place. Andy stamped around in his boots in front of the machine, got down on his knees and cleared the snow directly in front of the tread. He stood up, took a deep breath and started the engine. It started right up. Andy sighed with relief and turned the hand control. The machine edged forward, dropped lower a couple of inches, hesitated, then caught. Andy felt the machine steady as his foot found the lip of the road. Andy hitched the sections together and turned off the engine.

Taking off his wet gloves, Andy slapped them against the seat until they were free of snow. Then he opened the seat cover, took out the thermos, unwrapped another biscuit, and found his other pair of gloves. He took out his map, closed the seat and sat down. Andy knew he was close to False Canyon and no more than five or five-and-a-half miles from the turnoff to Nakoo's. He looked at his father's watch. It was quarter to nine. He had lost nearly a half hour overturning the machine. Looking up he realized the day was as light as it would probably get. A heavy gray haze hung overhead. He would hurry the next three miles, then slow down and look for the turnoff.

Andy gunned the engine and took off. Coming down a hill he saw the sign for False Canyon. Andy slowed the machine to crawl speed. He'd have to find the break in the trees.

He pictured how surprised Nakoo and Edna would be when he walked in. He hoped he and Nakoo could be on their way quickly, so they'd have a chance to find his father today. What was the checkpoint at the turnoff Nakoo had given him before? He couldn't remember.

Andy stood as he drove. Looking to the right he saw the river again, but no recognizable break. Then it flashed in his mind. The path was wide enough to drive a truck through, and about fifty feet down the trail on the left between the trees was an enormous squarish boulder. Andy also remembered that the river was back several hundred yards from the trail. Ten minutes later Andy came to a break in the trees. He stopped and walked off the road. No dirt road was under his feet, and he could see far enough ahead to rule this break out.

Easing the snowmobile forward, he resumed the same slow pace.

He spotted a second break less than a half mile later. Andy stopped the machine and walked through the break, sinking a foot into the loose snow with each step. Ten more steps and he stopped. The huge snow-covered boulder, like a silent sentinel, was there. Andy tramped back to the machine. He shut it off, opened the seat cover and took out his thermos and took a quick sip of hot chocolate. It had taken him two-and-a-half hours, but he was more than halfway to Nakoo's.

Chapter 6

Ray awoke in a sweat. The cockpit was warm even though the candle had burned out. He began the agonizing process of extricating himself from the sleeping bag. He would need aspirin quickly to alleviate the constant pain in his shoulder and throbbing ankle. He fashioned a sling for his arm from an oily rag that was thrown in the back. His foot presented a more difficult problem. He had managed to get his boot off last night. Now there was no way to get the swollen foot back in. He took the laces from his boot, put a fresh sock over his purple-colored foot, and tried to force his foot in. He couldn't do it. Then he tried to cut the upper half of his boot with his knife, but the toughness of the leather and his weakened grip made that impossible. Finally, he improvised, putting a second sock on, wrapping his foot in the extra shirt he carried and using the box his canned food had been packed in as a makeshift shoe. He used the lace to lash this contraption and enclosed it in one of the plastic bags he kept for trash and loose supplies.

An hour later Ray finally hobbled outside to survey the damage. His Cessna rested on the eastern slope of a mountain. Its propeller was bent, the left ski and support sheared off and the tip of the left wing was damaged.

Ray wanted to climb up on the wings and brush off the three inches of snow that covered them. It would make him easier to spot. But it was too slippery, and if he fell he couldn't take much of a jolt. Instead, he would cut a branch with his knife and brush them clear.

Ray was quickly frustrated. Less than fifteen feet from the plane, limping into the woods, he had fallen twice trying to pull his foot out of the heavy snow. His gloves were also wet. Ray looked up into the dark gray haze. It didn't matter anyway. There would be no rescue by air today. Impossible to fly in this soup. Ray looked back at the path the plane had taken after he had cleared the ridge. He had crashed about three hundred yards down slope. The plane would be screened from any land party searching along the lower elevations near the Ross River.

Ray struggled back into the plane, cleared his gloves of snow and put a new candle into the stove. He made himself a cup of bouillon and took more aspirin. He began to formulate a plan. He couldn't be more than twelve or fifteen miles from Nakoo's. In his condition he couldn't possibly get there, but he was sure if Father Dessault or his son got word to Nakoo, his old friend would come after him. He had to make it easier for Nakoo to find him.

For the next hour and a half, Ray prepared. He wrapped his sleeping bag, stove, candles, first-aid kit, flare gun, four flares, can opener, food and sweater in the canvas used for covering the cowling when he needed to warm his engine. Then he ate to build up his strength. It took an act of will to leave the comfort of the plane. He put on his baseball cap to shield his eyes from the falling snow.

The trek up the slight incline quickly tired him. Experimenting, like a swimmer trying different strokes to keep afloat, Ray stumbled forward until he settled into a rhythmical step-drag cadence, towing his supplies behind. The unnaturalness of dragging his foot forced him into a sideways motion. To keep from falling he had to keep his stepping motion short. Halfway to the top it began to snow. By the time he reached the crest of the ridge, Ray was gasping. Thick flakes were blinding him; he could see no more than forty yards ahead. What should he do? The trip back to the plane would take too long, and he would only have to try again later.

Ray stopped. He wanted to head right, in the direction of the river, but the ridge turned upward in that direction. The only clear path looked ahead, but leftward. Ray moved this way, looking for a place he could find shelter. The ground under him was uneven; the wind stung his face. After fighting his way along a craggy stretch of ground with dwarf pines on either side, Ray emerged at an opening where he could swing rightward and head downslope. Ray plunged a dozen steps and began feeling faint. Trying to move upward on one leg had exhausted him. A half hour's exertion had defeated him. He'd have to find a place to rest quickly. Fire and shelter would have to wait.

Lifting his cap to see better, Ray spotted a patch of jackpines. It took several dozen strides to reach them; he circled around to the right of the trees, looking for a boulder to shield him. He found one a hundred feet further along the level. Quickly he scooped out snow, creating a hollow against the boulder away from the wind.

Ray pulled the gloves from his cold hands and untied the canvas. He spread half of it on the ground, unrolled his sleeping bag on top, took off his jacket, boot and improvised foot covering and climbed in. He pulled the remaining canvas over himself and his supplies. His hands and face were very cold and his heart was beating hard. He gradually calmed down, knowing he'd be okay with a little rest.

Ray shivered. He was dizzy. Images of Sara floated into his consciousness. Then Andy. Why had he been so hard on his son? If he could take something back, it would be his blowing up at his son who was only thirteen when the tragedy with the dog occurred. He had lost control of himself when he found out that two drifters had killed Sammy with his rifle. What had he expected? He had allowed Andy to take the rifle. The men were dangerous. Nakoo had been helpless. Why had he blamed his son? Ray shook his head.

The snow fell steadily and warmth gradually returned. His mind cleared. Why had he belittled Andy instead of comforted him? There had been no excuse for that. He had failed Sara, and he was now failing his son.

Ray sat up and took two more aspirins from the

small bottle by his side. He put them in his mouth, then reached out and grabbed a handful of snow to wash them down. He choked, but swallowed them. Twenty minutes later he fell into a feverish sleep.

Chapter 7

Andy Ferguson put on his father's ski mask, adjusted the goggles over his eyes and smoothly started the snowmobile forward. It was only twelve or thirteen miles to Nakoo's cabin. He passed the huge boulder on the trail, shifting his body left, then right as the machine bumped over the uneven ground beneath. Trees were on either side of him; they seemed to absorb some of the snow. Then he came to an opening. He turned gradually left; he was on a rise with the Ross River on his right. The trail meandered beside the river all the way to Nakoo's cabin. Now the trees were only on his left. But he couldn't see as well because the falling snow was not blocked out by the trees. He began humming. He knew he had two creeks to cross ahead, but as long as he took his time he'd be fine.

Andy felt a surge of confidence. Nakoo and he would find his father. Almost everything Andy knew about his father Nakoo had told him. One of his best stories was how Nakoo had come to the Yukon and met his father.

Nakoo had once been a mechanic for bush pilots

in Galena, an airstrip near the Yukon River, a little more than a hundred miles from Unalakleet, a hamlet on the Alaskan seacoast where he had grown up. Nakoo's first wife had died, his daughter had moved away and his boss, who had become a drunk, had cheated him out of his pay once too often. With some money saved and nothing to hold him in Galena, he had decided to see the world. Like most mechanics who knew how fragile these single-engine planes were, he was deathly afraid of flying.

Nakoo felt his best chance was with an old geezer who had a good plane. Buzz Sawyer's plane looked like the inside of a junkyard, and the word was that Buzz took a bath twice a year whether he needed it or not.

"Well," Nakoo had said, "the old skunk nearly killed me. I hitched a ride with him from Galena. Twice he sneezed flying into Fairbanks; second time nearly took off the tower. That was enough. In Fairbanks, I ran into Mudhole, just before they grounded him. He was head'n for Dawson so that's the way I went. . . . Never got any further."

In Dawson, once the "gold rush" center of the Yukon, he went to a diner that was owned by a widow named Edna. He took a shine to her, wangled a job there and married her a year later.

That was where his father met Nakoo. His father, who was flying for Northern Air Charter then, was the only pilot Nakoo would fly with. When Nakoo and Edna decided to retire and sell their diner, they wanted to be near his father. Andy was glad. He could count on Nakoo and with Brian gone, he could tell Nakoo what was going on.

Andy kept the machine running a little faster than walking speed. The trail was uneven, but would be smooth for thirty- or forty-yard passages. A clearing opened in front of him. As long as the river was to his right, he should have no trouble. Too bad it wasn't December. The river then would be frozen solid enough to drive the snowmobile over it.

A patch of open river to his right appeared. He tried to keep the snowmobile straight. Ahead, he sensed movement. He slowed to a crawl and removed his goggles. Squinting through the snow he could see trees forming ahead and to his left. At the edge were . . . wolves. He stopped, counting six of them. They were watching him. Now was the time he needed the rifle. "Don't be afraid," he told himself. The wolves did not move. They did not seem threatening. Then he decided what to do. Taking the ax from its case, he held it over his head, let out a yell and gunned the snowmobile forward. If they didn't move, he would pass about sixty feet from them. Andy raced the engine but kept the machine steady. As he approached, the wolves unhurriedly began to trot away from him into the woods. As he passed the closest point, he stood up and saw blood on the ground. A partially eaten caribou laid there.

Andy slowed the machine and looked for the trail opening in the woods. The wolves had not followed. He put away the ax and made a half right turn, heading toward the river. He got off the machine and caught his breath. Had he continued ten feet further, he would have plunged over a steep embankment into the river. Andy shook his head. Sheer luck had prevented an accident. He looked back over his shoulder for the wolves. They were gone. Andy's main concern now was to make as much distance from them as he could.

He turned the snowmobile and cautiously resumed his journey. A few minutes later he was back on the trail. It had stopped snowing. Taking off his goggles, he pulled the ski mask up. He knew the first creek crossing was coming up soon. Three tree trunks lashed together spanned the creek at a narrow point. Andy looked at his father's watch. He was making good time. If all went well, he would be at the cabin before noon.

A half mile later, Andy crossed the creek and stopped. He drank the last of the hot chocolate from the thermos and checked the map. The next creek was about the same distance as this one had been from the road. Andy jogged in place to get his blood circulating. His toes and the tips of his fingers felt cold through his gloves.

The day was still dark gray as Andy pushed on. His thoughts returned to the second trip he made two summers back. He tried to block it out of his mind, but Sammy's image kept returning.

He had been so excited about the second trip that summer. They had flown out to Nakoo's, and his father had let him take his .30 .30. He and Sammy had bounded out of the plane, and raced to Nakoo's cabin. Nakoo and he and Sammy were taking an overnight trip to the end of Nakoo's trapline. Andy was going to help Nakoo work on the lean-to there. They were enclosing the open side, building a door and setting up a stove so Nakoo could use it during the winter when the weather turned bad.

Andy felt queasy about the traps, but he enjoyed the four-hour hike, except for the heavy backpacks. They reached the lean-to early in the afternoon, unpacked their gear and ate the lunch Edna had packed for them.

A half mile from the lean-to they found the poplars that Nakoo had picked out a month before. They had cut the first set of weathered trunks, roped them and began dragging them down hill. They had been working for an hour and a half. Within sight of the lean-to, Sammy suddenly bristled. Two men were rummaging around their packs. Nakoo shouted at them; they dropped the ropes and began running toward the men. Sammy snarled and raced ahead.

One of the intruders grabbed the rifle Andy had left propped against the wall and cocked it. He shot Sammy who was almost upon them. The golden retriever yelped, fell, struggled up, then collapsed at their feet. The two men ran off, carrying his father's rifle. When Andy reached Sammy, the dog had stopped breathing. He cradled the dog. Blood from the chest wound ran down his arms.

Andy sat holding the lifeless body of Sammy. Nakoo had tried to comfort him, but Andy could not stop crying. An hour later, after Nakoo had dug a grave for Sammy, they headed back. Nakoo would finish work on the shelter later.

Later that afternoon his father returned, landing on floats on the Ross River, and taxied up to the wood landing Nakoo had built. His father became very angry when he found out that Sammy had been killed with his rifle. He blamed Andy for leaving it back in the lean-to. Nakoo tried to calm his father down, but his father told Andy to pack his things, and a few minutes later they flew back home. That night, Andy again tried to explain what happened, but his father would not listen. Andy felt his father had never forgiven him. He wiped a tear from his cheek and spotted an exposed rock.

As Andy approached the second creek, he realized he would have to be careful. There was no log bridge here. Andy stopped the Bolin and checked the crossing; it was only twenty feet wide here. He could walk on the ice crust, but he didn't want to chance wrecking his autoboggan. He unhitched the back section of the Bolin at the edge of the ice. After walking across and testing the ice, he returned and quickly pulled it to the other side. Then, walking the heavier engine section across, he heard a crack, but managed to cross safely to the opposite shore. Andy rehitched the sections and moved upward on to the trail.

He pushed the machine faster now. His arms hurt and his body was sore from the vibrations and his ears were ringing with the constant roar of the engine. He had reached a plateau, winding in and out of scrub trees and rock formations.

Andy could sense he was getting close to the bridge Nakoo built over Big Timber Creek. He swung the snowmobile left, crossed a meadow and ahead saw the plank bridge over a narrow section of the creek. His spirits lifted as he crossed over and saw the cabin. Smoke was wafting upward from the stove pipe. He had made it.

Andy quickly shut off the engine and hurried to the door. When Edna opened the door, she smiled, but put her finger to her lips signaling to him to be quiet. Andy brushed the snow from his chest and took off his boots and laid them on the mat beside the door. There was a funny smell in the room. Edna pointed across the room. Nakoo was asleep.

"He's very sick," she whispered.

Andy's heart sank. Nakoo's face was thin and had a sickly yellow cast to it. His shallow breathing was uneven. Edna took him by the arm and led him to the table.

"What's wrong?" she asked.

"Dad crashed yesterday. North of here." He hesitated. "I came for Nakoo . . . I thought we could find him."

Edna patted him on the shoulder. "Andy," she said sadly, "Nakoo is too sick to even get out of bed."

Andy nodded. He took off his outer shirt and the sweater underneath and put his gloves on the stove. Confused, he finally blurted out, "I'll have to go alone." He paused and continued unconvincingly, "And I'll have to leave in a few minutes."

Edna shook her head. "I'll fix something for you, but wait until Nakoo wakes up." Andy agreed and went out to the snowmobile and brought in his map and thermos. They spoke in whispers for the next half hour. She made soup for him and had him sit by the stove and warm his feet while he drank tea. Andy looked at his watch. "It's twelve-thirty," he said, standing up. "I have to go."

"Wait," Edna answered. She went over to Nakoo and gently caressed his white hair. He stirred, and slowly opened his eyes. Edna whispered and the sick old man looked over and gestured for Andy to come over and sit on the side of the bed.

"Andy," Nakoo said in a weak voice. Edna helped her husband sit partially up, putting another pillow under his head. They told him about Andy's father crashing.

Andy brought his map over from the table and opened it. He showed Nakoo where he thought his father had gone down.

"Are you sure?"

Andy fibbed. "Uh-huh," he said, nodding.

"How far is it?" Nakoo asked.

"Only fourteen, fifteen miles," Andy answered.

"What time is it?" Nakoo asked.

Andy told him. Nakoo told him he couldn't possibly make it before dark. He would have to wait until morning. Nakoo smiled weakly. "Maybe, I'll be well enough to go."

Andy paused. "Nakoo, show me where the end of the trapline or where the shelter is." He unfolded his map and held it for Nakoo. Andy watched him feebly move his shaking finger, eyes watering, and realized that Nakoo could not see the small map markings. He patted the old man's hand, putting the map aside. "Just tell me."

Nakoo sank backward. Andy looked over to Edna who had a worried look on her face. The questions were too taxing for Nakoo.

"By the fourth lake . . ." he began, then closed his eyes.

Andy hesitated, then asked, "Is the stove in?"

Nakoo nodded. "Wood?" he asked in Nakoo's better ear. Again, the single nod in response. He patted Nakoo's hand.

Andy was shaken. Edna removed the pillow and helped Nakoo lie back. Nakoo was terribly sick. He took his map and returned to the table.

Andy lowered his head, pretending to examine the map, so Edna wouldn't see the tears that suddenly filled his eyes. It was impossible, he thought. When Edna went over to the stove, he pulled the drawing out of his other shirt pocket and laid it on top of the map. As he looked at the map and drawing, an idea came. If he could find the lean-to that he and Nakoo were going to enclose, he'd still have a chance to find his father.

Andy composed himself and ran his finger over the map, then looked up at Edna. "Aunt Edna," he asked, "have you gone with Nakoo on the trapline?"

She nodded. "This summer when Nakoo added the wall and door. Why?"

"Will you look at the map with me?"

Edna took a pair of reading glasses from her apron and looked down as Andy began to point out places to her. "Here's your cabin, right?" Edna agreed. "The trapline runs along this part of Big Timber Creek, then cuts up here." His finger pointed to a spot above where three lakes appeared in sequence.

"Andy," Edna said, "I'm not good with maps, but I think the end of the trapline is beyond the third lake. There's a stream nearby."

"It'd be about here I think." Then he moved his

finger up and marked between the third lake and one above it. "This is where Dad is," he added, running his index finger a little further up; it can't be more than six or seven miles from the shelter."

"It is close," Edna answered, adjusting her glasses, "you can go tomorrow morning. We'll use this afternoon to get everything organized."

"I have the snowmobile. I can be at the little cabin in two hours. I'll sleep there tonight, and it'll give me the whole day tomorrow to look for him."

Edna frowned. "It's too dangerous by yourself. No one's up there; you'll get lost."

They looked at each other. Andy looked over at Nakoo. "Aunt Edna, Nakoo won't be better tomorrow. I've got to go now. Dad might be hurt."

Edna shrugged. When she saw he wouldn't change his mind, she shrugged and began preparing things for him. She filled his thermos with soup and wrapped bread she had baked yesterday. Then she rummaged through several drawers by the bed and put Nakoo's scarf, flashlight and compass on the table. "Take these extra gloves, too," she said.

Andy watched her, then said, "Aunt Edna, I need Nakoo's rifle." She looked at him. "I'll need it to signal Dad," he explained.

Edna unhooked Nakoo's old single-action rifle from the wall by the door and began looking for cartridges. She found eleven in a box under the bed. Andy put them in his pants pockets.

Edna then got her coat and she gave Andy Nakoo's ax. "I've got an idea," she said. Minutes later they were both outside cutting branches from nearby trees. She wanted Andy to take markers so that he could find his way back to the shelter if he got lost. Andy didn't argue. It took them a half hour to strip branches and dip the ends in paint Nakoo had in the shed.

While Andy mixed and poured fresh fuel into the tank, and replenished the oil, Edna brought twine and tape from the cabin and secured the rifle and snowshoes on top of the markers. She cut a short piece of rope and tied it to the back of the snowmobile so they could drag the markers. Andy tried driving the snowmobile with the rifle, snowshoes and markers lashed behind. It worked without snagging. It was after two before he was ready to leave.

"Do you have everything?" she asked. He checked. He had Nakoo's compass and matches in one pocket of his wool shirt and the rifle cartridges divided between his front pants pockets. Everything else was packed, except for the flashlight she gave him, which he put in his back pocket. His father's bigger flashlight was in the seat compartment.

"I'll use the markers tomorrow morning," he said, "so anyone can follow me from the shelter. . . ."

Edna shook her head as Andy started the machine.

"I'm sorry about Nakoo," he said.

"Be careful, Andy," Edna said slowly, patting him on the back. "I wish you'd stay."

"I wish I could," he replied, as he turned the throttle and the snowmobile started. He headed toward Big Timber Creek, looked back once and waved to Edna, who had not moved.

Chapter 8

Fifty air miles east northeast of the Ross River settlement, an unnamed mountain rises four thousand seven hundred and fifty feet above sea level. Stands of white spruce and lodgepole pine trees dot its lower slopes between a thousand and twenty-eight hundred feet. Five miles from the summit, on a windswept western slope, the trees cluster in depressions between long barren stretches of snow-covered rock and scrub grass. On one such outcrop, just a rise, and just over a quarter mile from his plane, the battered pilot slept like a hibernating animal, huddled under a section of oil-smudged canvas.

The man stirred. It took several moments for him to get his bearings. The pain in his shoulder and ankle grimly reminded him of his predicament. He would rest for a few minutes before starting out again. This was his third crash. He prided himself that no passenger had ever been seriously injured with him. This time, though, he had nearly taken himself out. It was part of flying up here; something he learned quickly after leaving the States.

Ray Ferguson had been in the Yukon for seventeen years. A year after he returned from Korea, another veteran, Andy Drummond, who had been his flight instructor, helped him obtain his commercial license. After three years of flying rented or borrowed planes around the midwest, a friend told him that Northern Air Charter, a small company in Whitehorse, the capital of the Yukon Territory, needed a pilot.

Phil Olsen, the co-owner of Northern Air Charter, hired him the day he arrived. Phil had given him a crash course on Alaskan and Yukon weather and the Stinson he would fly for the next three years. Ray fell in love with the rugged, uninhabited country. When Phil Olsen was forced out of the company, he and his closest pilot friend, Eric Larrabe, quit and started their own company, BackCountry Air. Earlier the same year he had married Sara, a young woman he had met who worked in the Flight Control Office at the Whitehorse airport.

A year after they moved to Ross River, the small settlement a hundred and twenty air miles northeast of Whitehorse, young Andy was born. With his own plane, a new son, and Sara helping as the company's bookkeeper, the company began to prosper. Ray had never been happier. Then, when Andy was eight, it had all turned to ashes. While he was on a three-day trip to Anchorage, Alaska, Sara went into labor. By the time he had returned to the medical station in Whitehorse, Sara had lapsed into a coma and their baby daughter was stillborn. The next day his wife died. A part of him had died with her. He had to put the past aside now.

Ray lifted the canvas a couple of inches and peeked out; it had stopped snowing. He threw the canvas off, stumbled out of the sleeping bag and put his jacket on. His swollen ankle had turned an ugly purple and it took longer to construct another temporary boot. Ray felt weak, but more from hunger now. He would eat after he had built a shelter and started a fire. Working as fast as his cold hands and useless shoulder would permit, he repacked his gear.

Ray headed lower, angling westward toward the river. He wanted to find a spot where he could see and be seen. The sky was a dark, angry gray. No ceiling. An impossible day to fly. Sliding his left leg in front, he moved like a wounded animal, plunging awkwardly downhill. Falling forward with a lunge-drag, lunge-drag rhythm, Ray covered nearly two hundred yards before the stabbing fire in his right foot forced him to stop. Twice his frozen gloves had come off; they were nearly useless.

Resting for a couple of minutes, Ray scanned south and west. In the haze below he saw what appeared to be a cluster of sailing ships. Rubbing his eyes in disbelief, he staggered another fifty feet forward. Cradling his canvas-wrapped gear, Ray took a deep breath and headed for the high masts. Suddenly he fell into space. Ray dropped ten feet. somersaulting into two feet of snow. He landed on his back; his canvas roll clutched to his chest. So intent had he been in peering at the strange sight ahead that he had stepped off a ledge.

Tears came to his eyes as his shoulder screamed

its reaction. Then he began to laugh, crazily. Ray rolled over and stood up. Like a sportscaster, he announced: "Ferguson, somersault in pike position . . . degree of difficulty. . ." But no one was listening.

Turning, he saw what had looked like tall ships. In the gray haze were lodgepole pine trees that had been decimated by fire. He had seen them from the air hundreds of times; acre upon acre of forlorn, bleached poles, reaching skyward on denuded hills. He had come upon a stand of dead trees; the wood he needed for a signal fire.

The trees were over a hundred yards downslope. Ray headed toward them; he would circle around them and build a fire. As he stagger-walked toward the trees, images of the past began flooding his mind. He remembered sitting on the bed, telling Andy his mother had died. They both had cried. He felt tears in his eyes now. He could not remember how he flew with Andy and Nedda to the funeral.

Ray brushed the frozen tears aside, picked up the roll and began again — lunge-drag, lunge-drag — circling around the trees.

At last Ray was far enough away from the top corner of the stand to have a full view downslope and to his right. He began searching for a place to build a windbreak. The snow made it difficult to see. Finally he found a dip near the edge of a ridge.

For the next hour and a half, Ray worked like a man possessed. Crawling around, he scooped out snow and created a bowl-like hollow twelve feet wide. Then he limped back to the stand, and by feeling through the snow, found and dragged back small tree trunks and limbs. Finally he was ready to start a fire. With his energy fading, he searched for a few twigs or branches to serve as kindling. The two small pieces he found were not enough. Using his knife he managed, despite the fire in his shoulder, to peel a few shavings.

Ray found an old freight bill in his wallet. Using the canvas to shield the candle from the wind-blown snow, Ray lit it and then held it to the bill. Seconds later a small flame started on a peeling. Using his body to block the wind, Ray placed the peeling under a limb. Then he managed to light another peeling with the candle flame. Twenty minutes later he had a small fire. It provided little heat, but it would serve as a beacon.

Ray sank back, exhausted. There was not much more he could do. He roused himself and wearily made a tentlike cover with the canvas. Propped up by bare branches, it blocked the wind and snow from his sleeping bag and a corner of the fire. It would have to do for now. He was too tired to do anything else. He managed to heat a can of bouillon as he lay in his sleeping bag next to the fire. His eyes began to glaze after he had taken a few sips.

"Come on, Nakoo. Come on Nakoo," he said aloud to the unhearing wilderness.

Chapter 9

Andy felt like a zombie. The shock of finding Nakoo in such pitiable condition numbed him. He wanted to stay with Edna and Nakoo. They were his friends. He wanted to go back to the warm cabin, but his body acted independently. Everything was muddled.

Could he find his father without Nakoo? It was impossible. No it wasn't. After all, the plane couldn't be that far from the end of the trapline. It was possible. He had a rifle, too.

Andy stopped the snowmobile and looked upward into the heavy grayness. Then he looked at his father's watch. Less than two hours of light. He had made an important decision at Nakoo's. He was not going to follow Nakoo's meandering trapline that wound eastward near the Big Timber Creek several miles before turning north. It would take too long. No, he turned and circled behind the cabin; he would head north, hugging the right shore of the Ross River and then cut across between the second and third lake. It would save at least four miles and he should be able to make it in an hour. He had two compasses to help him. He would use them and set some markers on the way.

Andy took out the map and checked, then he turned the throttle and slid forward. The roar of the machine drowned out his thoughts as he moved lower to a sandbar. It was only three miles to the first creek that ran from a lake into the river. He would stay as close to the river as the terrain permitted. The land now was marshy, but the snow-crust held. He bumped along until a rock formation blocked him. Andy planted a marker than turned upward to high ground and planted a second marker. No sense worrying about the river, he thought. If he headed straight north according to the map he would run into the creek. Andy stopped, stepped away from the snowmobile and checked Na-koo's compass. A skull-shaped mound ahead was slightly left of north. He moved in and out of the scrub, and as he passed the mound saw the creek below. A light snow began falling. Andy pulled his ski mask and goggles from under the seat. Maneu-vering the machine in and out of the trees, he came to the creek's edge. He lifted the goggles. The creek was more than twenty feet wide.

Andy planted a blue-tipped marker, then headed upstream away from the river. The ice should be better this way. He stopped and gingerly stepped on to the ice. It was white and sounded hollow. Nakoo had warned him about shelf ice. He moved another hundred yards upstream where it was nar-rower and tried again. There were animal tracks crossing the creek here. Andy knelt down, brushed away the snow and tapped the ice. It sounded more solid. He walked across the creek, following the tracks. Okay. Hurrying back to the snowmobile, he threaded his way back to the water's edge, then sped across. Andy exhaled in relief as he planted another marker. Checking the map he saw that the second creek looked to be only a mile or so north. It also connected with a lake. No need to run near the river, he'd use the compass and head straight north again.

Was it getting darker or were the trees blocking out what little light there was? The thought sent a shiver of fear through him. Weaving in and out of trees, Andy hurried northward until he came out onto a meadow. Checking the compass, he planted another marker and sped across. A rabbit darted away nearby. It wasn't any lighter in the open.

The next run was uphill. Reaching a crest, he stopped and planted a marker. The dip below was too steep to try and continue northward. A minute later a craggy outgrowth blocked him. He was forced to swing back and down a long bumpy hill before he was finally around the obstacles. He checked the compass again to get his bearings. It was very difficult now, trying to thread between trees and keep northward. Finally, he came out onto what Yukoners called muskeg, a level swampy expanse of ground. Planting another marker, Andy sighted a lone, rectangular boulder ahead he could use as a marker. When he reached it, he caught sight of a water break ahead to his left.

Andy quickly reached the creek and stopped. Hungrily he swallowed some of Edna's soup, choking momentarily on a carrot. As he ate a piece of the bread she had wrapped, Andy took out the map, spread it, and using his flashlight, located his position. A new idea came. If he followed this creek eastward to where it flowed out of the second lake he could save even more time. Swinging around the right side of the lake would put him about two miles from the third lake. From there he would be very close to Nakoo's trail and the shelter. Yes, that's what he'd do.

Andy's adrenaline was pumping. After placing three markers to show his new direction, Andy cautiously guided the machine along the south side of the creek. No need to cross it if he could find its source. The dim light seemed the same as he moved in and out of the brush. Gradually he could feel the terrain changing. He was moving upward and the creek had narrowed. There were more water breaks. Twice he slowed to circle boulders. Creeping along, the slope became steeper and he had to pick his way between spruces and avoid rocks.

So intent was his concentration in the winding ascent, he failed to notice the ground had leveled until the lake appeared in front of him. He was at the south end of the tooth-shaped lake he had noted on the map. Stiffly, he stood up, planted two more markers and stepped out onto the snow-covered lake. The ice held him. As far as he could see, it looked smooth and peaceful. He could save precious minutes by riding on the lake, arcing around the eastern side and getting off at the northern end. He checked the map, which had been perfect so far. The southern tip of the third lake was about two miles north above the upper corner of this one. He stuffed his ski mask into his back pocket.

Jumping on the snowmobile, he turned the throttle and the machine leaped onto the lake, went out fifteen yards from shore and sped eastward. Two hundred yards later, following the curve of the shore, he angled the fast moving autoboggan northward. They were flying forward at twenty miles an hour when he heard a snap. The ice held. Andy eased shoreward and was only twenty feet from shore when a thunderous crack sounded.

He turned directly to land. The machine churned under the snow, stopped as if hitting a wall, and Andy catapulted over the top. For a moment he was flying, then he landed face first in freezing slush, his chin grazing undersnow gravel. Plowing through the wet snow, his elbow, chest, and knee banged hard against the ice. He sprawled on the ground by the lake's edge, the wind knocked from him. Ice water drenched him. Stunned, Andy could not breathe. He stumbled wildly to his feet. Floundering in the dark haze he finally gasped some air. Then retching snow and soup, he turned and watched helplessly as the engine section sank into the water. He shivered uncontrollably.

Where was the seat section? Andy spun around and found it a few feet from him, on its side, against an exposed tree root. Quickly he pushed hard, righted it and pulled it fully onto the shore. Andy was wracked with convulsions. His upper body was heavy with water-sogged clothes. His shaking hands pried open the seat latch. Everything inside was dry. He tore open his wet wool shirt, but couldn't pull it over his hands. Frantically, he peeled off his sodden gloves and yanked his shirt free. His sweater and inside thermal shirt clung to him; he grunted and toppled over before wriggling free of them. Something gooey and warm was on his hands. Blood. His chin was raw and open. But he couldn't deal with it now. Drying his chest with his father's sweater, he put on his father's thermal undertop and wool shirt. He wrapped the wet sweater around his waist. No time to change his pants. The scarf Nedda made was lying there. He wrapped it around his neck, tucking it against his chest.

Andy stopped. Where was the rifle? His snow-shoes? Grabbing his father's big flashlight, he flipped it on and swung it back and forth. It was nearly dark. He jumped up and down, slapped his hands together, then rubbed them and put his father's gloves on. Andy tried to steady his hand as the light beam swung back and forth. Moments later he found the rifle, lying in its brown wrap on shore, about eight feet from where the back section had been. The twine connecting it to the seat section had snapped, but it was still wrapped around the trigger guard. Andy had no knife. He returned to the seat compartment and using the ax blade freed the twine; he also cut the rope that had dropped the markers behind. He needed the rope; the markers were useless now.

The snowshoes had to be close. Edna had used separate twine on those, but had taped them on top of the rifle. The light beam crisscrossed the darkness. They weren't on the ground. God, he was freezing. Where were they? On the lake? Andy shifted position, standing on the spot where he had found the rifle. He turned the flashlight back toward the lake. Half the engine section was now submerged. He stepped around a tree to see better, and the light fell on where the seat section had skidded. His eye caught something. Dangling from a low overhanging spruce branch was twine. The light snowshoes had entangled on two low hanging branches.

Andy quickly removed them and tied them to his boots. It was dusk. Andy found the thermos and started to drink the soup. He coughed up the first mouthful. The inside of the thermos had shattered. He poured hot soup on his hands, brushing away glass fragments. He wolfed down a couple of carrot and meat chunks and threw the thermos aside. In a dry sock he found three cookies Nedda had packed; he ate them quickly. Then he pulled his father's yellow poncho from the bottom of the compartment, and fashioned a backpack. Before tying it down, he moved the second compass and matches from his wet wool shirt pocket to his father's dry shirt pockets, and retied his wet sweater around his waist. Andy fumbled open Nakoo's compass. He checked for north. Had he damaged it? He pulled his father's compass from the dry shirt pocket. No, it was okay. Both showed north the same way. Andy went to the edge of the lake to see how far he was from the northern tip. He couldn't tell. He'd have to travel along the edge of the lake until the compass told him to head north. Gathering his gear, he awkwardly started to walk. Five minutes later he reached the northern edge of the lake. He kept stumbling, trying to get used to the snowshoes.

Shifting the rifle to cradle position he began to stride uphill, away from the lake. The shivering lessened. Twice he stopped to adjust the bindings of his snowshoes. If he headed about five degrees east of north, he should walk directly into the third lake. Andy felt numb and heavy; he began to trot to get warm and make time. He had to use the flashlight to see ahead and check his compass.

Andy's mind was blank as he half trotted, half shuffled. He could not think about what had happened. For stretches he was able to see clearly enough to shut off the flashlight. Twice when he checked the compass, he found himself drifting right. Andy's chin stung and his ears were getting cold. The ski mask and Nakoo's flashlight were gone. He pulled the scarf up over his head to cover his ears. He dabbed his chin with a handkerchief. The lower half of his body had not gotten as wet. His knees were sore but only a little water had gotten into his pants and boots. Where was the third lake? He felt he had gone far enough.

Andy stopped. With only his flashlight, compass and ax, he started westward. He took off his jacket and draped it over a boulder. Then a few minutes later, he was able to mark a pair of trees on either side of him. But he had lost count of steps. Had he come one hundred or two hundred? It'd be okay. He'd take four hundred more steps.

Andy had started westward because he was certain the lake had to be this way. He had trouble even coming close to maintaining a straight line. He stamped his snowshoes to make his tracks deeper. After counting four hundred steps, he stopped. No lake. He'd try one more hill and look down on either side. He carefully marked his way to the next crest and looked around. He shook his head in despair; he had been so sure. The snowshoe tracks helped him find his way back. It was seven o'clock by the time he returned. He had made a plan, but now he felt it wouldn't work. The lake couldn't be in the other direction. No sense going the other way. Maybe he hadn't walked as far north as he thought. Andy sobbed. He knew he couldn't walk all night. He was too cold and tired. Gathering his gear, he repacked everything and grimly headed north. He made up his mind to walk north until quarter to eight, then try to locate it again. In the back of his mind he kept expecting to walk right into the lake. It was closer to eight P.M. before Andy found another high hill to use as a base.

Hurrying west again Andy shuffled six or seven hundred paces with the same result. Was finding a lake in the dark impossible? He groaned. The flashlight was growing dim. It was almost nine when he had returned to the hill where he left his gear. He had not stuck to his plan the first time. This time, even though he felt it was wasting what little strength he had, he'd go eastward. If nothing turned up, he would make a camp close by and sleep.

Andy clomped along, his legs quivering with fatigue. His mind was empty. He had crossed a hill and traveled about three hundred paces when he heard a car engine. He hurried forward; now it sounded like fast running water. With his flashlight weaving light in front of him, he saw a swift running brook up ahead. But the sound was not from here.

It was coming from above. He followed the stream upward and the sound grew louder. He was having trouble now; it was getting steeper, but the roar of water was deafening. Andy removed his snowshoes, and grabbed trees and brush to help him climb. He came upon a waterfall. Andy scrambled past it to the top of the hill where the water was plummeting over. To his amazement a big lake lay in front of him.

Andy was dumbfounded. Where was he? Andy retraced his steps back down the hill, put his snowshoes back on and followed his trail back to where he had left his pack and rifle. He was confused. He took out the wet map and tried to figure out what had happened. Carefully, he unfolded the wet map and laid it out on the ground. Part of the map came apart in his hand. With his flashlight jittering in his hand he found the third lake. No stream showed where he was. But the fourth lake did have a stream flowing out of the south end. He checked his drawing. It showed the same thing. Andy's mind went back to the trapline trip he had taken with Nakoo. A creek paralleled Nakoo's trapline over the last two or three miles. Could this be the source? The shelter was about two hundred yards east of it. He and Nakoo had washed their cooking utensils in it. Andy got to his feet and checked the watch. It was now after ten. If this was *that* creek and he followed along it, keeping the right distance, he should walk right into the lean-to that Nakoo had enclosed. Andy quickly returned and repacked. Heading back along the creek, Andy walked a quarter of a mile before climbing a hill. The compass confirmed that he was heading south, the right direction. He would lose sight of the creek, but he had no choice. He and Nakoo had not traveled to the lake he had just found, but he did remember his friend saying that another lake was about a mile from the lean-to. After he had walked another ten minutes, he checked to see where the creek was. It seemed about the right distance to his left. He cut back, heading south, hoping, hoping. There was no sense walking more than a half hour.

It was difficult just lifting one foot after another. The snowshoes felt like lead weights. He was in a daze as he crossed over the next hill and started southward again. He waved the flashlight left and right in front, hoping something would appear. He moved in and out through spruce trees, then came out into a clearing. He was swinging the dim light back and forth when the dull beam of light caught something different to his right. He swung the flashlight over. It was a snow-covered woodpile and next to it was the log shelter.

Was it a miracle? Or dumb luck? Wearily, Andy took off his snowshoes and propped them near the door. Opening the door latch, he collapsed into the tiny cabin. The flashlight dimly swept over the few items inside: the small barrel stove, a tree stump with an old sleeping bag sitting on it, and a plank held up by logs that Nakoo used for a table. A few empty cans and a rusty cup sat on it. Behind the cans Andy found two candles and a box of matches. Andy quickly lit a candle and shut off the flashlight. He wedged the candle between two of the cans, then went outside to get wood. Getting warm was the only thing that mattered now. Andy brushed snow from the top of the pile and pulled out a half dozen small logs and dumped them inside. He returned for a second load. There was no kindling so he cut shavings from three of the split logs and opened the stove door. Two inches of ashes were inside. He took the candle and held it under the shavings. He put two of the smaller logs across and waited. The fire caught, but smoke poured out. Andy coughed. Using part of the poncho, he fanned the opening until the smoke reversed and went up the stove pipe.

Andy's eyes were burning. He fixed the candle in a soup can and reached for the musty smelling sleeping bag. He felt sick and headachy. No. One more thing to do before he rested. He switched the flashlight on again and saw an old jacket hanging from a nail hook. He took the jacket off, then strung his rope from the nail over the stove to the other corner. He hung his wet wool shirt and his sweater over the rope. He put two more logs in the stove and laid his gloves over the barrel. Then he took off his boots and climbed into the sleeping bag, and pulled his supplies near him. He pulled the jacket over him. He looked blearily at the fire in the stove before his eyes closed.

Chapter 10

The howling wind woke Ray. Pulling the zipper of his bag down, he saw the fire had gone out. It was not snowing, but a drift had formed against one side of his fragile windbreak. He had no idea of the time, but guessed it was the middle of the night. After he was up and dressed, it took him two hours to make five trips to haul enough wood back for his fire and shelter. Crawling around the twelve-foot hollow he cleared more space with his good arm, then using a candle and his knife to create kindling, he finally restarted the fire . He had tried to shield the fire from gusts of wind but had been too weak to move the rocks that seemed locked into the ground around him. He had managed to drag a few logs over to create a partial windbreak. The canvas had come loose during the night. He anchored it again. If it didn't snow anymore, the fire might last till morning. Ray climbed back into the sleeping bag, feeling more helpless and miserable than he could ever remember. His sleeping bag was as close to the fire as it could safely be. He kept a bark-stripped branch within hand's reach to feed the fire one more time before morning.

Ray lay there wide awake. His usually clean, angular face was dirty and grizzled. Fingering his stubble he mused. Last week he had remembered sitting one night at home, paging through the new issue of *Flying* magazine. Andy had been looking at him. Ray was certain now that Andy had wanted to say something, but he had certainly not invited conversation. In fact, he had not had a real talk with his son since he had blown up over the rifle incident.

That incident had resurfaced this past fall. He had flown a mineral expert from Mayo over to Norman Wells in the Northwest Territory. After he had secured the plane, he and his passenger John LeConte had stopped for dinner in the saloon there. John was good company, and Ray was usually fascinated by John's stories about the silver and zinc explorations he supervised. But that night, as they finished dinner, Ray's attention had been diverted by two sleazy-looking men who were drinking at the bar. He had been straining to pick up their conversation when the taller of the two men pulled an emblem from his pocket that he wanted to exchange with the bartender for a drink. They fit the description that Nakoo and Andy had given him of the men who shot Sammy. Ray was sure the emblem was an old one he had given Nakoo that Nakoo had hooked on his backpack.

Without thinking Ray leaped to his feet and angrily grabbed the emblem off the bar before the startled bartender could respond. Wrenching the long-haired man by the shirt collar, he snarled "Where'd you get this?"

The tall, scraggly man tried to pull away. His sidekick gripped Ray's shirt, flashing a knife. Fortunately, Ray's dinner companion saw what was happening, and caught the other man before he could turn the knife on Ray. Ray lashed out in a fury. He punched the man he had grappled with in the face, knocking him to the floor. In the scuffle a chair, dishes and several glasses had been broken. The bartender and several of the regulars hauled the two drifters outside, restored order and calmed Ray down.

The encounter had taken less than two minutes. Ray would have spent the night in jail, had it not been that the owner of the place refused to press charges, and the mountie who had been called in had suspected the two of preying on old trappers in the area, but did not have enough evidence to support it. There were also hundreds of emblems like the one he had given Nakoo. Ray felt sure they were the two. What he had to show for it was a broken knuckle, a torn shirt and a one hundred and fifty dollar bar bill.

Ray lay there on the cold, hard ground. Why had he reacted so poorly? The fight had solved nothing. Nakoo had even told him later he needed to make amends with his son. He knew how Andy felt about Sammy. Why hadn't he apologized? Ray shook his head. Was he any better than his own father?

Ray tried to shut off his mind. His thoughts instead drifted to how he could get out of here. What if his radio transmission hadn't been heard? It didn't matter. Ernie would still report him missing after four hours. Then what? They had no way of tracking down Billy John. Even if Father Dessault could drive his van up the North Canol Road, his arthritic knees couldn't take the rigor of searching the rough, snowy terrain. Nakoo had no way of knowing he was down. He couldn't walk out. Ernie or Father Dessault would think of something. At least it hadn't turned cold.

Ray took three more aspirins and ate half of his next-to-last can of corned beef. Then he reached out his good arm and carefully placed the branch by his side across the burning logs. Don't snow, he commanded and tucked his head into the sleeping bag.

Chapter 11

In the dream Andy could not wake Nakoo. The two drifters who had killed Sammy were in the cabin. Andy tried to shake Nakoo and then woke in terror. The candle was flickering in the blackness. Something was in the tiny cabin with him. He pulled his hand from inside the sleeping bag and felt around for the flashlight. He found it and switched it on. Two mice were nibbling at what was left of the bread Edna had packed. He sighed, relieved. When he had opened the poncho-pack, the bread wrapped in waxed paper had come partially open.

Andy yelled at the mice. They had gobbled more than half of the bread that was left. The mice skittered off in the darkness. Andy looked over at the stove. It was warm in here, but the fire was almost out. He rolled to his knees and turned the stiff gloves over, loaded the stove again, and used a shaving to reignite the fire. After the flame was steady, he shut the door almost closed so the wood would burn more slowly. Andy's body felt sore and the muscles in his legs were twitching. Crawling around, he readjusted the damp clothes on the rope line. Then he ate a can of salmon that Nedda had packed. Nedda made him hot chocolate with milk at home. For now he'd make do with powdered chocolate in water.

The stove created a circle of warmth in the tiny cabin. Moving his boots close to the stove, he hoped the wet clothes would be dry by morning. His father's watch read 2:12; he wound it. The frantic night trip had taken everything out of him. He prayed for good weather. Andy could go no further. His chest hurt from hitting the ice, his right elbow and knee were skinned and his chin ached constantly. He had no medical supplies. In the morning he would put snow on his chin; maybe that would numb the sting. It wouldn't be light till nine; he'd get more sleep now.

Two hours later Andy thrashed awake. Viselike spasms gripped his legs. Sweating and screaming, he rolled out of the sleeping bag and tried to get to his feet. Cracking his head on the low roof he fell back again, furiously rubbing the cramping muscles. After ten minutes of writhing and rubbing he felt the cramps gradually subside. But for the next twenty minutes his legs still twitched, the muscles contracting. He was afraid to curl up in the sleeping bag again so he got up and lit the other candle. Moving about, rearranging the damp clothes and bringing in more wood helped to relieve the cramps.

Andy turned the flashlight on and looked at the wet, worn map. It was hard to make out the markings now. Using a twig he estimated how far it was from the shelter to the "x" he had marked. It looked less than seven miles. He was going to have to try. If his father were somewhere between six and eight miles, he could get there well before noon. If he couldn't find him, he could return to the shelter by dark. Andy wiped the rifle dry and checked the trigger. It clicked. But what would he do without markers? He'd have to think of something.

Andy rolled the tree stump over near the stove and sat with his back against it and his legs outstretched in front of him. The stove had made the little shelter so warm now, he could sit in his thermal underwear. Wisps of fresh air came from under the door and from small chinks in the walls.

For a moment, Andy sat there feeling sorry for himself. He had gone out for basketball this fall. The coach, his gym teacher, told him he could shoot, but that he would have to "grow up and put some weight on" and then come back. He wasn't good at anything. Andy thought about the story Nakoo had told him about his own grandmother. When Nakoo had been a young boy growing up near the Alaskan seacoast, his old, sickly grandmother felt so worn out and feeble one icy February night, she waited till everyone was asleep, crawled outside of their igloo to a nearby mound and froze to death. What happened if you were young and useless? He thought of the snowmobile sinking into the lake.

Andy rubbed his eyes and took out the map again. Half the distance to the "x" — a little to the east — was a mountain that stood nearly five thousand feet. He wondered if his father could have crashed into it. It seemed too far east of the route he was flying. It made no difference. Andy had come at least forty miles; he would have to go the rest of the way. Andy clenched his fists; one way or another he would finish this. Opening the stove door, he put another log on the fire. Then he yawned and climbed into his sleeping bag. He stared upward in the darkness for a long time.

It had only seemed like moments, but the watch read ten after seven. Too early to start. He adjusted his gloves and clothes around the stove, then dozed for another hour. Andy had never felt so sore as he struggled from the sleeping bag. His chin was raw. His socks and gloves were dry and flattened. Andy ate, packed his gear and checked the map. He began to feel better.

He opened the door. It was still dark, but it was not snowing. Andy spread the damp map out, and, using the big flashlight that had regained some brightness, traced his path back to the lake he had found last night. He would cross that lake, then head north-northeast to where he had marked the "x." A huge mountain nearly five thousand feet high would be off to his right, and about a mile before the marking he would cross a creek. After that he would find a hill with good visibililty and fire the rifle.

A half hour later Andy drank two cups of watery hot chocolate and adjusted his poncho pack. Even though he had no thermos, he took the tea bags and hot chocolate. He packed these in a small can he had scoured. Andy made a final check of critical items; he had everything, including Nakoo's sleeping bag. Outside the sky was slightly lighter. He put his snowshoes on and began walking over the spongy ground slowly; he wanted to work out the stiffness and pace himself. His coordination was poor; he felt like he was wearing tennis rackets on his feet.

Andy heard the waterfall a few minutes later. He walked onto the lake. After he recovered his breath from the uphill ascent, he walked briskly along the fringe of the lake. By the time he reached the northern tip he knew he had covered over two miles. It had gotten a little lighter, but it was very gloomy and overcast.

The mountain on his right was immense. He could not see the top. As long as he kept it to his right and held a compass setting of about fifteen degrees he should be fine. Andy was moving into higher country, and he had difficulty keeping near the setting because he had to weave in and around scrub. Andy longed to see something to break the monotony. Except for the wolves he had seen before arriving at Nakoo's and the rabbit afterwards, he had not seen anything move. It was so silent all he could hear was the scrunching sound of the snowshoes and his own breathing. Each time he reached a rise, he made markers, often using stones he had to pry loose. He began feeling the futility of this effort. He stopped and rested twice, ate the last slice of bread and continued the trek.

By ten Andy was already tired. He couldn't be far from the creek now; he took the map he had drawn and checked it. Despite the necessity of circumventing obstacles he was sure he had come more than five miles. The ground was becoming more craggy and uneven. Andy decided to swing up and around what seemed an endless stretch of spruce trees. He climbed above them, looking for a ridge that he could continue northward on. A steep incline forced him to take off his snowshoes and climb until he reached an open stretch of rock and scrub. Lacing his snowshoes back on, he zigzagged northward until he came to a hill that gave him almost a quarter-mile visibility on all sides. He stopped and rested. Each stop now, he had to shut off the mocking voice in his head that kept telling him that the search was stupid.

Even though the next stretch was more downhill, Andy could feel his legs getting heavier and heavier. He began talking to himself, and was so oblivious to his surroundings, that he almost walked into the creek. A water break a few feet in front alerted him. The stream was narrow here, not more than twelve or fifteen feet wide. Andy found a smooth section, quickly crossed, and followed the creek eastward and upward again to clearer high ground. Again, he found it easier to clamber, hunched forward, without his snowshoes.

Twenty minutes of steady climbing brought him to a level expanse of open ground. Andy put on his snowshoes and sighted northward. A steep hill began forming in front of him; it was too sharp to climb directly. Instead, he circled around the right until he reached the far side. A few minutes later he found a crest that gave him a fairly open view on two sides. Andy brushed snow away from a boulder and sat down. He ate the remainder of the canned salmon, and then loaded the first cartridge into the chamber of Nakoo's rifle.

He had made up his mind to fire his first shots now, but he only had eleven shells. His father had once told him that the international rescue signal was three shots fired at ten-second intervals. He'd need time to reload the single-shot rifle, but he decided he couldn't waste that many shells. Andy put the rifle to his shoulder and fired. The sound surprised him as much as the jolt to his shoulder. Taking his time, he counted five seconds after reloading and fired again. Listening intently he slowly scanned the dark haze around him. Nothing.

Andy sat down and rested until he could feel the wet coldness penetrating his long johns. What should he do? Andy could feel his strength ebbing away. Next time he fired he wanted a better view. He decided to head higher, more eastward. He resumed his plodding, trying to keep an easy energy-saving rhythm. Ten minutes later, he came to a ridge that appeared to follow a northeastern slant. He followed it and finally came to a crest that gave a view on three sides. He walked around it, then gave himself orders like a soldier. He fired, and a moment later heard a muffled sound to his left. He hurried to that side of the hill and saw below a herd of twenty or thirty caribou bounding into the woods. Putting his rifle upward, he fired again and waited. Discouraged, he put his backpack back on and decided to follow the deer.

With each step Andy knew he was jeopardizing his chances of returning to Nakoo's trapline shelter, but it was easy following the caribou tracks that headed in the general direction he felt he should go. A half mile later he spotted them again; this time they veered northwest, but he decided to turn eastward toward a rise that was forming to his right. Just as he reached the ridge line it began to snow.

Andy's legs were getting wobbly. His backpack tired him. With no ski mask or goggles, he pulled Nedda's scarf from under his shirt, and brought it up to cover his hair and ears. His chin ached. He fingered the shells in his pocket — seven left. The snow was still light, but gusts of wind blew it up and around him, and he could see less than a hundred yards ahead. Andy trudged along for another half an hour until he came to the summit of a ridge. Mechanically, he removed his backpack, and fired twice. Snow clumped down from the trees above and to the left of him. Andy waited and watched, then leaned against a tree. Opening his pack, he took out the small can and mixed chocolate powder with snow. It tasted good. It was near noon and he didn't know what to do. Last night had taken too much out of him. He could never make it back to the shelter. He wanted to find a spot where he could make camp. But it was too early.

Fifteen minutes later, clumping downward along a rocky slope that headed into some jackpines, Andy found a ledge that jutted outward, offering protection from the falling snow. Andy scrambled underneath, unhooked his poncho-backpack, unrolled the sleeping bag, took off his snowshoes and boots and crawled into the ragged quilt. He would rest for a few minutes.

Two hours later Andy jerked awake. He rubbed snow into his eyes. He had a confusing dream about Charlie and encountering wolves. Andy lay for minutes trying to think clearly. Should he cut back west and head for the river and the possible safety of the North Canol Road? No. He had five cartridges left. He would go a little further, shoot, then decide. At least it had stopped snowing. He wrapped his gear in the sleeping bag and put on the yellow poncho.

The terrain ahead looked better heading slightly west of north. After several minutes he was threading his way up and down through scattered spruces and poplars. He tumbled and wearily got up. He would walk until three, then find a knoll, and fire again. A massive formation of rock blocked his path ahead so Andy turned eastward and began the slow ascent up and around. The ground was very uneven and his snowshoes clanked together. Andy fell, then fell again getting up. Even though he had rested, he was panting as he plodded upward in a daze. Now his gloves were wet.

Maneuvering in and out of a patch of jackpines, Andy finally reached a rocky hump of ground with three table-sized boulders. He took off his pack, cleared the smallest boulder, put his gear down and took two more cartridges from his pocket. He put the cartridges between his teeth and rubbed his hands together until his fingers lost their numb feeling. He fired and didn't count, reloaded and fired again. He had a difficult time focusing his eyes as he looked ahead and to his right.

Andy had scanned the horizon twice before he realized that there was a dull pink haze in the overcast above and to his left. It took a moment for him to realize that it might be a flare. The pink faded. He gathered his pack, forgetting his tiredness, and plunged ahead. His heart was racing; he would go toward where he had seen the glow and then fire the rifle again.

Chapter 12

Twice during the night Ray made the painful trek to the trees. Each trip was further from the windbreak and more tiring. Trying to drag back the roped-together limbs and keep his balance forced him to stop every few feet. After each grueling excursion, Ray ate half a can of corned beef, fixed himself a cup of bouillon and took two aspirins. He slept fitfully in between.

When daylight finally came, the sky remained an ugly dark gray. It was still socked in. His condition was worsening: the makeshift foot binding was too tattered, the plastic wrap shredded. It was imperative to keep the fire going; it was the only chance that someone would spot him. By mid-afternoon Ray had made three more trips for wood. Now he alternated a fresh sock on his ankle with a shirt wrapped around.

Once he heard the faraway drone of a high-flying plane. By the time he struggled to his feet, it was too far off. It was probably an airliner or military plane flying high above the weather that made low-level VFR flying impossible. As the day wore on, he grew more and more convinced that his emergency transmission hadn't been heard. He was down to one candle now. He resolved to keep the fire going until dark; he knew he couldn't keep it going another night. If no one came, he'd try to work his way back to the plane in the morning.

Ray was in a stupor. Dozing fitfully, he imagined he heard a distant rifle shot. More awake, Ray lifted his head. Was that a second muffled report? Groping for his flare gun, Ray held it shakily skyward with one hand, and pulled the trigger with the other one. There was a thunk and the sky above turned red for ten seconds. Ray stumbled out of the bag and staggered to his feet. Fumbling around, he loaded a second canister and readied a third. Ten minutes passed, twenty, and just as he decided he had only imagined the sounds, a much closer rifle shot broke the stillness.

Ray raised the flare gun and fired directly overhead. Nothing happened. He discarded the canister, put the other one in and fired again. Moments later, the red glow flooded the gray above. Another shot rang out, much closer. Ray peered intently downslope and to his right. His shoulder was on fire with pain. When he saw nothing, he tore one of the protective logs from the break, and laid it across the fire. Then he tore the canvas free and tried to fan the fire. The useless exercise only intensified the pain in his shoulder. He limped back and peered downward.

In the haze he heard movement. Ray yelled as loud as he could, "Nakoo, Nakoo . . . up here." He heard movement to his right below him. Out of the haze a tiny yellow figure appeared, heading toward him. Ray wiped his ice-crusted eyebrows, straining to see the single approaching figure. He could make out the yellow poncho of the climber who was using a rifle like a ski pole to climb upward. He waved and called out again, "Nakoo?"

The figure waved back and Ray heard, "It's me, Dad."

"Andy!" his father exclaimed, as his son closed the distance between them. Hobbling around the lip of the hollowed outbreak, Ray stumbled on his son's snowshoes and embraced him. Ray shook his head unbelievingly. Andy dropped the rifle and took off his snowshoes.

"Where's Nakoo?" his father asked.

Andy caught his breath and helped his father back into the hollow. "He couldn't come; he's very sick." Then he looked down at his father's half-bare, swollen foot. "C'mon, we'll have to wrap that." Andy helped his father down on his sleeping bag, quickly pulled Nakoo's sleeping bag from his back and let the gear fall out beside his father. "For now, wrap this around your foot," he said, circling the foot with Nakoo's sleeping bag.

"How did you find me?"

Andy shrugged. He couldn't think what to say.

"Amazing . . . amazing!" his father repeated. Ray hugged Andy. They moved closer to the fire. Ray touched his son's face. "What happened to your chin? The skin's raw."

"It's a long story, Dad," Andy replied.

Ray shifted through his gear and found the first-aid kit. Squeezing some ointment onto his finger, he delicately spread it onto his son's open wound.

Andy winced.

His father handed him the aspirin bottle. "I've been living on these," he said. "They'll help the pain." Ray handed Andy an empty can.

Andy took off his gloves, laid them over two of the cans and pushed them near the fire. "I'll get wood after I warm up," he said. They sat in silence as darkness began to envelop them. Andy looked at the tired, battered body of his father and at the smoldering fire. "Where did you get the wood?" he asked.

Ray pointed. "You'll have to go further in; I've taken all the deadfall from this corner."

Andy helped his father back into his sleeping bag. With his ax, he made two trips into the stand. Ray watched his son rebuild the shelter and bring the fire back up. They agreed that Andy should make one more trip to keep the fire going during the night. Ray dozed while his son worked.

After Andy finished, he woke his father and handed him tea he had heated for him. Then they shared the last can of corned beef. Andy rearranged the floor of their shelter. He put the canvas more under his father, and spread the poncho half above them to shield them from the wind and snow. Andy took the watch from his wrist and strapped it on his father's.

"You forgot to take this with you," he said. Four hours had passed. After they moved the sleeping bags, they sat, half sitting, and Andy asked what happened.

"I guess the fuel line clogged . . . hard to say. I

barely had time to give my position," his father answered.

"Where's the plane?"

"On the other side of the rise," Ray gestured above them, "in much better shape than me."

"Why'd you come over here?" Andy asked.

"I knew it'd be tougher to find me over there, and I figured Nakoo . . . would try to find me. I never. . . . How did you find me?"

In bits and pieces Andy told his father all that had happened from the time Father Dessault gave him the message. When he came to the part about losing the snowmobile, Ray could tell his son was upset. Ray patted him. "Forget it, son," he said. "If you hadn't found me, I might not have made it through the night." After Andy finished, they sat for a few minutes in silence. Then Ray spoke, barely above a whisper. "You're lucky to be alive," he began. "You took a terrible chance, coming alone. Very brave. Very brave."

"I'm not brave, Dad." Andy haltingly told his father about Charlie, about getting beat up, about being scared at school.

His father listened intently. "Why didn't you tell me?" he asked after a long pause. When Andy didn't answer his father sat up and looked at him, and finally mumbled, "I'm sorry . . . it's me . . . I haven't been around."

Andy did not know what he meant.

His father kept shaking his head, kept patting him. He was groping for words.

"I hated my own father," he said firmly. "He left my mother, sister and me when I was twelve. I had my own trouble with bullies, two of them the next year . . . got beat up pretty good — "

"How'd you get out of it?"

"It's hard to remember that far back," his father answered, "especially something that awful." But then a faint smile crossed his face. "You know, I do remember the last time one of them picked on me."

Andy had found his father's knife and was cutting shavings as his father talked. He waited for his father to continue; put down the knife and pushed a half-charred log further into the fire. "What happened?" he finally asked.

"Sure you want to hear this?" his father asked, frowning. "No one's ever heard it." Andy nodded. His father took the ointment he had given Andy for his chin and gestured for Andy to rub some more on while they talked. "All right," he continued. "My mother sent my sister and me on an errand . . . to a shoemaker. My sister had the shoes in a bag. We had gone about three blocks, when this big kid who had been beating on me came up to us. . . . He never looked at my sister, just pushed on me like he had done before . . . and my sister pulled the shoe out of the bag and cracked him in the skull with it. Before he could do anything, she cracked him again. He ran off. . . . I don't ever remember seeing him again."

They both laughed. "You're kidding, Dad!"

"I swear it's the truth," his father answered. "How 'bout making us something to drink?"

Andy took his gloves off the two cans that were sitting by the edge of the fire, and began scouring them. "Tea, okay?"

"I prefer coffee," his father replied, "but tonight I'll settle for tea."

"I wish we had sugar," Andy said.

"We might have. Try my jacket pocket."

Andy crawled over and felt around the jacket pockets. In the left one he found three sugar packets. He held them up for his father.

His father clenched his fist and sighed. "Don't worry about that bully; we'll take care of it when we get home. . . ."

Twenty minutes later they had their tea, but not before Andy had burned his fingers on one of the hot cans. They waited until the cans cooled and then drank the tea with their gloves on.

"Get some rest, Dad," Andy said as they watched the fire burn steadily.

Andy zipped his father's bag up further and tucked his scarf under his father's head. He moved some logs around, making sure there was enough air space underneath so that the blaze wouldn't die down for a while. Then he laid back in Nakoo's bag, and huddled close to his father.

Chapter 13

Andy awoke well after midnight. Something was very different. The fire was nearly out. He'd have to fix it quickly. He looked up at the sky. He thought how his father had never told him anything about his own father before. Then he knew what was different. As he stared up into the night, he could see stars. It was very clear. And very cold. The weather had changed. He'd have to move quickly. After Andy climbed out of his bag, he had trouble starting the fire again. Using his father's knife and his own dulled ax, he managed to cut more shavings and with the help of a candle the fire sputtered to life. He moved some smaller branches in place to keep it from going out. His face was so cold now he could hardly breathe. There was no wind. It had to be near zero. Or under. He sat as close to the fire as he could but could feel no heat.

Andy was going to have to find more wood later because the few branches here were burning fast, and he couldn't let his father get out of his bag. The cold went right through his gloves. If they didn't freeze to death, someone should come in the morning. Working quickly, Andy removed two logs from their windbreak, then chinked snow into the gaps of their frail half-moon shelter. He grabbed the flannel shirt from his pack and wrapped it around his face and ears. He whispered in his father's ear, "Keep your head in the sleeping bag. Don't get out, Dad." After splitting and breaking the two logs, Andy stacked them carefully on the fire and huddled next to his father, trying to keep warm.

It was after six when his father's movement woke Andy. He explained what had happened. The situation was desperate. His father was fully awake now; he looked at his watch and said, "If we can hold out for a few hours, help will come." He was sitting up. With his good arm he fumbled around until he found his gloves. He handed them to Andy. "Wear both pairs," he said. "Build up the fire, but don't stay out for more than twenty minutes at a time." He gave Andy the scarf and had him wrap a flannel shirt around his neck and ears.

Andy understood. It was too cold to even take the time to put his snowshoes back on; it was hard enough to force his stiff boots on and lace them up. With ax in hand, he tramped through the foot-deep snow further into the stand of lodgepole pines and spruces. The exertion of getting to the trees kept Andy warm for the first few minutes, then the knife-like cold cut through his wrappings. The snow was too deep to search along the ground; he also couldn't risk getting his double gloves wet. His eyes darted around the bare trees. He pushed against several dead-looking thin pines until one gave; a minute later he found a leaning trunk half caught in a spruce. He dragged them back through the heavy snow.

"Climb into your sleeping bag," his father told him, taking the smaller of the two logs.

"After I split this one," Andy replied, seeing his father trying to work with one arm. With his father's foot holding the log, it took more than a dozen slashes with the ax before the dead trunk broke open. Once split, it was easier to break the limb into two. His father built up the fire while Andy took off his boots and climbed back into the sleeping bag. Both sets of gloves were damp now. Andy shook for minutes until warmth slowly returned to his body. His father had him turn his sleeping bag with his head near the fire.

"Rub this on your face," his father said, handing Andy a shirt he had warmed with the fire. Then they drank hot chocolate in the bone-chilling darkness. At least there was no wind.

With agonizing slowness dawn finally came. With the first light they crawled out of their sleeping bags. Ray Ferguson heated cans of snow-water. After ten minutes of intermittent arm-wearying chopping, Andy cracked the thin trunk of the other tree and laid it across the fast burning logs. There was almost no heat from the fire even though they had enclosed more than a third of the hollowed-out space.

"Should I go again?" Andy asked his father.

"Just grab one trunk," his father answered, looking up; it was lighter now than it had been at any time the last two days. "Before you go, let me show you how to use this," he said, passing the flare gun to Andy. Ray showed Andy how to load the canister. Then he had Andy warm his face again and gave him the driest pair of gloves. Andy put on his snowshoes this time. He couldn't make his mind work as he trudged toward the trees.

It was nearly ten when Andy came back uphill, dragging two stripped limbs. They heard the sound at the same time. Not the steady purr of an airplane engine, but the rhythmic chop-chop sound of a distant helicopter. Andy dropped the wood and shuffled back to camp. He was taking off his snowshoes when the sound faded. Ray told him not to worry; the pilot was probably flying a pattern. As soon as they sighted the copter, Andy would fire the last flare.

Ten minutes later they heard the sound again. Finally a black speck appeared southwest of them. Andy pointed the flare gun upward and fired. Nothing happened.

"Forget it," his father yelled. "Fan the fire." Andy yanked the yellow poncho free and whipped it up and down. A tiny wisp of smoke floated skyward.

The sound of the helicopter grew louder. Appearing over the horizon, the brown military copter flew above the creek Andy had crossed yesterday and on away from them. The sound began to fade; then they heard it again gradually become stronger. The copter was coming back on the other side now. This time it was closer. Andy handed his father the yellow poncho, grabbed two shirts and began running around, yelling and waving. The low-flying helicopter passed, then banked sharply and headed toward them. Andy jumped up and down and waved as his father yelled. They could see the corpsman next to the pilot. He waved back. The deafening noise increased as the chopper circled, looking for a place to land.

Two minutes later, it settled down fifty yards upslope. Andy acted as a crutch for his father as they staggered toward it. The blowing snow cut their faces. The Plexiglas door opened and the corpsman jumped out, grabbed Ray and helped him into the cabin. Andy went back with the corpsman to their shelter. They kicked snow on the fire and grabbed the gear, throwing it into the canvas and poncho, bundled them up and hurried back to the machine.

Five minutes later, the engine roared to life and they were airborne. The corpsman gave Ray a cup of hot coffee, but he was shaking so hard, he splashed half of it in his face. Ray grimaced and slumped backward. The corpsman helped him with the coffee, then removed the shirt from Ray's foot. He looked from Ray to Andy, and asked, "We know who you are. Who's this?"

Ray smiled. "My son, Andy."

"How the hell did he get here?" the corpsman asked.

"He came overland," his father replied. Andy grinned.

"Where's your plane?" the pilot asked.

Ray directed them over the ridge and the chopper dropped lower, turned twice, then hovered over the nearly invisible aircraft below. "Doesn't look bad," the corpsman said, as he opened the door and dropped a sack of red dye earthward.

"Where you from?" Ray asked the pilot.

"Comox," he replied. "We followed the storm around. We were in Whitehorse yesterday, tried to get out twice, but couldn't see a thing."

"It's good you got here when you did," Andy said.

"We'd've been here earlier, but it took over an hour to get the chopper ready. It was five below zero when we cleared Whitehorse."

The corpsman said something they couldn't hear to the pilot, and the pilot leaned back. "We're going back to Whitehorse. Doctor there. You need some attention."

Ray nodded and closed his eyes.

The corpsman introduced himself to Andy, handed him coffee and asked, "How did you *really* get here?"

Andy took a sip of the coffee and looked down at his father. "I started out with a snowmobile" — he paused — "but I lost that in a lake." He shrugged, unable to find words.

"See what happens when you don't leave it to the pros," the corpsman quipped. He covered Andy's father with a blanket. "Damn kids," he added with mock contempt.

Andy smiled.

The helicopter gained altitude and headed southwest over the frozen land.

point

Other books you will enjoy, about real kids like you!